D1571932

GUN TRUTH

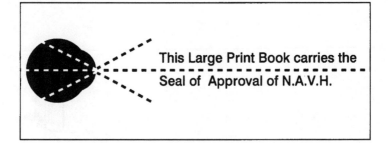

GUN TRUTH

ED GORMAN

Thorndike Press • Waterville, Maine

Published in 2004 by arrangement with
Leisure Books, a division of Dorchester Publishing Co., Inc.

Thorndike Press® Large Print Western.

The tree indicium is a trademark of Thorndike Press.

The text of this Large Print edition is unabridged.
Other aspects of the book may vary from the original edition.

Set in 16 pt. Plantin by Ramona Watson.

Printed in the United States on permanent paper.

Library of Congress Cataloging-in-Publication Data

Gorman, Edward.
    Gun truth / Ed Gorman.
      p. cm. 344 23
    ISBN 0-7862-6444-6 (lg. print : hc : alk. paper)
    1. Sheriffs — Fiction. 2. Deception — Fiction.
    3. Triangles (Interpersonal relations) — Fiction. 4. Large
type books. I. Title.
PS3557.O759G86 2004 03
   813′.54—dc22   2004047918

Here's one for Tom Piccirilli.

As the Founder/CEO of NAVH, the only national health agency solely devoted to those who, although not totally blind, have an eye disease which could lead to serious visual impairment, I am pleased to recognize Thorndike Press* as one of the leading publishers in the large print field.

Founded in 1954 in San Francisco to prepare large print textbooks for partially seeing children, NAVH became the pioneer and standard setting agency in the preparation of large type.

Today, those publishers who meet our standards carry the prestigious "Seal of Approval" indicating high quality large print. We are delighted that Thorndike Press is one of the publishers whose titles meet these standards. We are also pleased to recognize the significant contribution Thorndike Press is making in this important and growing field.

Lorraine H. Marchi, L.H.D.
Founder/CEO
NAVH

* Thorndike Press encompasses the following imprints: Thorndike, Wheeler, Walker and Large Print Press.

CHAPTER ONE

You couldn't pick up a newspaper these days without finding an article or editorial about how barbed wire had changed everything out west. Some were for it, some were agin it.

It was 1886 and people were still arguing about it. Some said it made good friends; some said barbed wire made blood enemies.

Al Woodward was agin it. While it was fine for ranchers and farmers and livestock breeders, it was hell on insurance investigators.

Take tonight.

Al Woodward, a freelance insurance investigator for several different companies, had been climbing through some barbed wire when one of the barbs tore the right buttock of his new trousers. And dug a painful little trench of hot blood across the same buttock.

But Al was more worried about his trousers than his buttock.

These weren't your Sears & Roebucks or

your Monkey Wards at $1.49. These were $3.98 trousers bought at one of the best men's stores in Chicago, purchased only two weeks ago.

Al cursed himself for wearing these tonight. Damned barbed wire.

Now that he stood upright, his hand unconsciously favoring the rip in his trousers, he looked around at the large round lake whose surface shimmered with moonlight, some of the shimmers even playing off the scrub pines that encircled three sides of the water. Pretty as a painting of a lake at nighttime, but —

Damned barbed wire. And damned stupid dime-novel melodrama. Meeting out here. There wasn't anyplace closer to meet?

Al Woodward was in town working on an arson case. He'd been here two days now and had just this afternoon started putting the scheme and the person responsible together. The local fire folks, amateurs at best, hadn't seen any evidence of arson. But to Al it was obvious. He'd talked to some people who lived near the small factory, and the way they described the fire, there wasn't much doubt that it had been set by human hand. He'd even found two pieces of two-by-four that had been scorched in a way that indicated kerosene.

Al had also turned up a man who claimed — by letter — that he had been paid to start the fire. He'd found the letter late this afternoon in his hotel room. Pushed under the door.

The letter contained a map of the lake here, and how to reach it, and the time to be there and meet the arsonist.

Well, here was pants-torn Al . . . where the hell was the man who'd summoned him?

He heard a distant noise from the town of Claybank. He responded instinctively by turning his head in that direction. And when he did, he saw the object on the narrow band of sandy shore that ran around sixty percent of the lake.

He had a pretty good idea of what it was, which was why he hesitated at first to tromp over there for a closer look. He wasn't a brave man and never pretended to be. When saloon friends boasted of their courage, he kept his mouth shut. He was no hero.

What had moments before been a lovely scene of moonlight-limned pines and lake had quickly become a deserted and sinister collection of shadowy crevices, forbidding woods, and a body of water that held God knew what.

He was for that instant a child again, afraid of the dark because of all those stupid ghost stories his cousin Purvis was always telling him when he stayed overnight. Even at seven years old, he'd recognized those stories as so much bushwah. But they scared him nonetheless. (He was a suggestible boy, just as he became a suggestible man, unable to read any medical articles because he came down with every disease he'd ever read about, totaling, by now, six bouts of leprosy and something like forty-one heart attacks.)

He had to go over there and see what the hell was lying on the shore. Even from here, it was obvious what it was. But maybe the person was still alive. Maybe there would be something Al Woodward could do to help him.

He didn't hurry.

And he kept moving his eyes around, looking for the merest sign of life. Maybe the man had been felled by an animal. Or maybe been bitten by a snake. Or maybe simply had a heart attack like one of the forty-one heart attacks he himself had had.

But then again —

It didn't take an Edgar Allan Poe to come up with the idea that maybe the man (and the closer he got, the more clearly the shape became a facedown man) had come out here to meet Al and was then met by the man he was going to snitch on. And the snitchee killed him.

Happened all the time. Al, right off the top of his head, could think of six or seven incidents like this working out of the Kansas City office alone.

Arson was a serious charge, especially when it involved, as this case did, the death of a man who'd been trapped inside. The man had been a late-night worker who'd been trapped in the flames because they engulfed the building so quickly. Now, maybe the arsonist hadn't planned on killing anybody — probably hadn't, in fact — but that didn't matter. A man was dead, murdered. First degree, second degree, manslaughter. That would be up to a jury to decide.

The man wore a tan twill shirt and tan twill trousers. The kind of clothes, almost uniformlike, that workmen in the city had started wearing.

His elbows were cocked on either side of him. His feet were in the gently lapping dark water from about the top of the ankle on down. He had dark hair, small ears, wide shoulders, slender hips. There was really nothing remarkable about him at all.

By this time, Al Woodward was on his haunches. He gaped around because he had this feeling that somebody was watching him.

That darn Purvis.

He had a terrible thought: Maybe he was going to pee his pants. Wouldn't that be something? At his age? He'd peed them right in front of Purvis one night. Humiliating.

Al really didn't have time to register much but pain. The man came up so quickly — right up from the beach like somebody who'd been buried alive — and locked his hands on Al's throat so forcefully that Al felt his life choking away immediately.

Al's eyes began to pop. Blood imbued his cheeks with an ugly redness. Sweat beads like transparent warts covered his forehead. Saliva began to erupt out of him. His nostrils ran with blood. His false teeth flew out and hit his killer in the face. Far from being annoyed by this, the killer only laughed, as if the false teeth had been a part of a joke.

The killer had thought this through.

His next move was to spin around — taking Al with him — and push Al into the dark lapping lake itself. Noise of water splashing furiously. Noise of Al making strangled screams in his throat. Noise of the killer breathing hard. This wasn't easy, not easy at all.

And then the killer baptized Al unto death. Held his head under water until Al had ceased his useless thrashing, his faint, would-be cries.

The killer spent only a few more minutes with Al, roping twenty-pound blocks of iron onto each ankle and then swimming the corpse out to the middle of the lake, where the water was at least thirty feet deep and numbingly cold.

For a long moment, Al bobbed on the surface of the lake, a sad puffy figure painted gold by the moon, and then the water around him began bubbling and his sightless eyes addressed the earth for the last time.

The vortex took him then.

CHAPTER TWO

On the sunny morning of October 4, 1886, Deputy Tom Prine saw the man for the third time in three days.

The man was middle-aged, on the beefy side, in a rumpled dark suit that tried hard to make him look respectable. But the broken nose and wary eyes and large, busted hands suggested a rough life lived on the edges of the law.

Prine saw all this from his window table in The Friendly Café, which was half a block down from the sheriff's office. Yesterday, he'd walked past the man, close enough to register various details.

Prine himself was a slender twenty-nine-year-old with an angular face that many women found handsome in a melancholy way.

As evidence of this, Lucy Killane, the freckle-faced redhead with the gentle brown eyes and the sweetly erotic face, said to him now, "D'you know about the band concert tomorrow night, Tom?"

"I saw some posters for it, Lucy."

"I'm planning on going. And you could always stop by for supper early if you wanted to go with me."

Prine wished now that he'd never gone out with her. By the time he started to pull away, after four months of courting, he seemed to have let down not just Lucy but the entire town. She had been orphaned when she was six and raised by the nuns at the convent. They had instilled in her gentleness and a selflessness that never asked for reward of any kind. She just liked helping people, whether at the hospital, the church, the park where the old folks gathered.

Prine had had his share of romances. He'd always felt good about breaking off before he lost control of the situation. Men liked to act tough where females were concerned, but he'd known a lot of men who walked around brokenhearted because of some little gal in some distant town they'd fled to mourn alone.

But with Lucy, it was different. When he saw the pain in her eyes now, he felt no glee, no romantic triumph. Here was a good, true, forthright woman. Not a saint; nor did she pretend to be one. She liked beer and naughty jokes, and on a couple of nights she'd almost given in to him completely. But she was an honest and honorable friend and would never desert him. He had put that pain, that mourning, that sorrow in her eyes, and he damned himself for doing it. A lot of his girls had liked the game of love as much as he did. But not Lucy. Her feelings were simple and transparent and deep.

The terrible thing was — the thing that had caused him to turn away from her — was that he wanted more. She worked in a café and he was a deputy. Even between them they couldn't earn enough money to live anything more than a hardscrabble life. A tiny shacklike house somewhere. Three or four kids running around. And a sameness — day in and day out — that would be as crushing to him as any prison could ever be.

He'd known a deputy once who'd courted and won the hand of a rich girl. The man now lived in splendor and relative ease. The girl's old man helped him learn the cattle business. And now the former deputy was on his way to becoming cattle-rich himself. Prine never told anybody about this. It'd make him sound like a moony young kid, some stupid magazine-story dream of hitching up with a rich girl. But it was a flame that burned with the tireless brilliance of a votive candle in the most secret part of his heart. He couldn't extinguish that dream even if he wanted to.

He looked up at Lucy now, hovering there, trying to smile with that small lovely Irish mouth. But there was no smiling to be found in those sweet eyes. Just the terrible loss that Prine had put there.

"Try me again sometime, though," Prine said.

"Sure."

The tears in her voice and eyes were unbearable.

He slipped his hand into hers.

"I'm sorry about it all, Lucy."

He glanced around, seeing if anybody was watching. Fortunately, nobody seemed to be. A scene in a café wouldn't be good for either of them.

"I know you are, Tom. I don't blame you."

"Maybe if it was a couple of years down the line, when I was more ready for —"

And then she laughed, a rich sound he'd always loved.

"You don't have to come in here, but you do. You don't have to be nice to me, but you are. You don't have to let me embarrass you, but you do. You're a good Catholic, Tom, and you're not a Catholic

17

at all — but you've sure got the guilt like one."

He smiled, squeezed her hand, then removed his.

"I've got this book I read every night. *How to Be Guilty and Like It.* It's teaching me a lot."

Her moment of laughter was gone. "I'm thinking of moving, Tom."

"Not because of me, I hope."

A tiny smile. "Not because of you. You're not the center of my universe anymore, Tom Prine. I'm thinking of moving to get meself a better job and meet some new people." She always said "meself" instead of "myself." The last vestiges of a brogue she'd picked up from her long-dead parents.

Prine was surprised by his reaction. He felt — abandoned. It was ludicrous, stupid. He'd broken off with her. But now she was talking about leaving.

Before he could say anything, she said, "There's a customer waving for me, Tom. I'd better go."

Abandoned. Yes, that was exactly how he felt. It was one thing to break it off with her, but another to think that she'd be gone from his life completely. . . .

He went back to studying the man across the street.

18

What made Prine curious, as he sat there on his midmorning coffee break, was that every morning the man did two odd things. He would suddenly pull out his railroad watch and check the time. And then he would write something in a small notebook he took from his back pocket.

Only this morning did Prine see what spurred the man to take out his pocket watch and tablet. And that was the appearance of Miss Cassie Neville in her fringed buggy. Cassie was the daughter of Cletus Neville, a rich mining man who before his death had divided his estate between Cassie and her twin brother, Richard.

Now, there was an obvious reason for any man to watch Cassie. She was a dark-haired, dark-eyed beauty of grace and style. Twice a year she went to Chicago frock-hunting. And three or four times a year she traveled to St. Louis to hear their famous symphony orchestra. She had been engaged four times and she was only twenty-two years old. Needless to say, it had been Cassie who'd broken off the engagements.

Fine and dandy.

A smitten man, even a middle-aged fool, had every right to place himself in position to watch Cassie as she came to town five days a week to work in the basement of St. Francis Catholic church, where she taught school and handed out provisions to the poor. The Nevilles paid for all the provisions. A lot of townspeople donated clothes and used toys and housewares.

Fine and dandy. To just watch the young beauty in her buggy was one thing. But to clock her and then to write down the time — at the very least, that was a strange thing to do three mornings running.

Prine decided to find out what the man was doing.

Karl Tolan had been in jail enough — never prison; that was his street-boy pride, never prison — to recognize when a lawman came within thirty yards of him. Tolan could sniff one out the same way a hunting dog can sniff out a bird or a fox.

The man sitting in the window of The Friendly Café was definitely law. This was the third morning he'd watched Tolan watch the Neville girl, and this morning — or so Tolan sensed, anyway — the lawman seemed to get a sense of what was going on here.

But the three mornings had been worth it. He had the information he needed.

By the time Prine reached the street, the

man was gone. Prine hurried up and down the street, but there was no sight of him.

Five minutes after leaving the café, Prine walked into the sheriff's office. He knew instantly that Mae, the sheriff's spinster daughter, had cleaned up last night. The sweet scent of furniture polish was in the air.

The one-story building was divided into two parts. The office was large enough to hold four desks, an oil stove, three wooden filing cabinets, and several rifle racks mounted on the wall. There was a NOTICE board with current Wanted posters — current because this was another job Mae did.

Sheriff Wyn Daly looked up and said, "Coffee any better this morning?"

Prine shook his head. "I sure wish Peggy hadn't retired."

"People your age just don't seem to make good coffee," Deputy Bob Carlyle said.

Prine laughed. "I get the impression you don't think people my age can do much of anything."

Carlyle surprised him by saying, "Well, you're a pretty fair deputy, Prine. I'd have to say that."

Wyn, white-haired, beefy in the tan twill

uniform they all wore, looked up and said, "I don't believe I've ever heard you hand out a compliment in the eight years you've been here, Bob."

"Well, it's true. Prine here's good at the job." This was coming from a scrawny man of fifty or so whom too many drunks had underestimated because of his somewhat slumped posture and one glass eye. He had a quick hard right hand that had put down nearly every street tough in town.

Wyn laughed. "Be sure and write that on a calendar somewhere, Tom. October 4, Bob Carlyle gives somebody a compliment."

The rest of the morning went pretty much that way. Sort of slow and chatty. There was a fourth deputy, Harry Ryan, but he was the night man. A morning like this gave the day people a chance to talk over open cases, most of which ran to minor rustling, minor arson, minor saloon violence, minor theft, minor burglary.

The emphasis being on minor.

In a town of 6,700 — in a town that cattle drives bypassed, a town that was essentially one big general store for a lot of smaller surrounding towns — you didn't expect a lot of trouble. There had been three homicides and one bank robbery last year.

There was a portable gallows stored in the courthouse. Sheriff Daly had had to oversee the hanging of one of the convicted killers. Though the state legislature had made it next to impossible for gapers to attend hangings, many lawmen made a big event of hanging anyway. Hell, you had towns where they *advertised* their hangings. Turned the damned thing into a carnival — literally, with a horse race, games for the kids, a pie-baking contest, and a barn dance in the evening.

Wyn allowed as how he was grateful that the legislature was now considering making prisons responsible for all executions.

Prine and Carlyle brought Daly up to date on what they planned to do the next few days. Prine generally worked the north side of the map and Carlyle the south. This included town and approximately forty miles out.

When he wasn't talking or listening, Prine kept thinking about the man outside the café these last three days.

Just after noon, he started looking for the man. The obvious places were the two hotels. Nobody seemed to know who he was talking about. He next tried the main boardinghouses, of which there were four. Same result. Hadn't seen such a man.

He was just about to start on the houses where only a man or two boarded. There were a lot of them — maybe ten — and it would take some time.

He had started on the third such house when he happened to look over his shoulder and see something that rattled him.

The man he was looking for was following him. And he was pretty damned bad at hiding it.

About all the man could do was start swinging his head from side to side as if he were looking for a particular address. Then, ridiculously, he started whistling in order to give the impression that he was just out for a stroll on this mild autumn day when the scent of burning leaves lent the air a nostalgic aroma.

Prine was about to approach him when he heard the whistle. The sound emanated from a small steam device that Sheriff Daly used to pull in his deputies for an emergency. The sound was unlike any other in town, so a deputy couldn't say he confused it with something else. Pity the deputy who didn't respond to it.

Much as Prine wanted to talk to the

man, he had to turn in the opposite direction and run back to town.

The emergency turned out to be a grain wagon that had overturned on a railroad crossing. The wagon was full. Not only was there grain heaped across the tracks, but the driver was pinned beneath. He didn't look good. For sure many bones, including his ribs, were broken, but he was also bleeding from his nose and mouth. Prine was no doctor, but he knew that death was in the air, hovering.

Took four men to right the wagon. A buckboard stood by to rush the man to the six-bed hospital. Prine rolled himself a cigarette and listened to Daly and Carlyle and nighttime deputy Harry Ryan talk about that poor sonofabitch probably wasn't going to make it. And they were right. He was dead when they lifted him from the bed of the buckboard.

In the late afternoon, Prine broke up a saloon fight, arresting one of the fighters. He also found a missing puppy and helped an elderly lady who had locked herself out, forcing open a back window and climbing inside to unlock the door.

Early dusk, a marvel of purple and gold and half-moon in the sky, and the scent of winter on the air — early dusk, and Prine sat in his window seat in The Friendly Café, putting away a good meal of meat loaf, corn, green beans, and apple pie.

Thinking about the man who'd been watching Cassie Neville three days running.

What the hell was the man up to, anyway?

CHAPTER THREE

Two days later, Prine resumed his canvassing, looking for the man he'd seen noting Cassie Neville's arrival in town each morning. The smaller boardinghouses — two-, three-roomers, no more — rarely received the kind of upkeep the large ones did. The large ones were set up like hotels, with meals, washing privileges, mail set aside, and parlors and porches where the boarders could spend their nights in a homelike fashion. These houses generally catered to workingmen, especially unmarried railroad men, who were frequently gone half a month or so and didn't want to spend their money on renting anything bigger or fancier.

The smaller houses catered more often to transients. Prine remembered reading after Lincoln's assassination that cheap boardinghouses "were dreams for assassins and unholy people of every stripe." You take a big city like Washington, D.C., for instance. You had so many boardinghouses there, searching for one man was damned near impossible. He could keep moving, for one thing, and so the search became a shell game of a kind. Now he's here, now he's there. Impossible.

Claybank wasn't big enough to have such rabbitwarrens, but it still took Prine most of an afternoon to go to every house that advertised rooms, a list he'd gotten under the ruse of "official business" from the newspaper.

With three houses left to go, a weary, wiry woman named Wilma Chambers said, "That sounds like Mr. Tolan." She had a goiter on her neck the size of a baseball. It was hairy and tufted-looking. He'd never seen anything like it and didn't want to again.

"You know his first name, ma'am?"

"Of course I know his first name." She made a clucking sound that indicated that one of them here was pretty damned dumb, and it wasn't her. "Karl."

"Karl Tolan. Thank you. You probably know what he does, then."

"What he does is come and go. And pays his rent on time. That's all I know and all I need to know. The mister, when he was alive, always told me not to answer any questions from the law unless they told me why they were asking. Has Tolan done something?"

"Not at all. We just check sometimes on people who stay in Claybank for a while."

"He done something, didn't he? He hurt somebody? Is that it? He hurt somebody?"

"Ma'am, listen. I'm telling you the truth. We run checks on people passing through just in case something *does* happen. That's all, and that's a fact."

"Uh-huh. You boys with the badges think you can get away with anything. I'll tell you one thing, though. He gives me any trouble — tries to molest me or kill me — I'm gonna sue this town for every penny it's got. You know right now that he's a rapist or a killer. Or maybe both. But you won't tell me, will you?"

"I appreciate your time, Mrs. Chambers. Thank you."

As he was walking down the front steps, she said, "You remember what I said. I'll sue this town for every damned penny you've got, you hear me?"

There was an empty lot directly across the street from Mrs. Chambers's. Just after dark, Prine climbed up in the large oak on the far edge of the lot, moving fast so she wouldn't see him, and waited for Karl Tolan to come home. He had to take a chance that Tolan wasn't already home.

The autumn leaves were just full enough to hide him well. The only way he could pee was to lean forward and splash it down the back side of the tree. Several times, he wanted to roll a cigarette but decided he'd better not. At one point, a couple of teenage boys came along. Wouldn't it play hell if they decided to climb the same tree he was in?

What they did was sit under the tree and share a corncob pipe and argue about which girl at school had the biggest breasts. They both had favorites and they were both adamant about those favorites. (Kids determined to indulge in the forbidden pleasures of the pipe are oblivious to such things as a thirty-two-degree temperature. The debate went on for some time, during which Prine froze his balls off.) The argument ended when one of the boys decided to throw faces into the mix. He might concede that his friend's favorite had bigger tits by a smidgen or two, but if you figured faces into the mix — big tits *and* a pretty face — well, then, there was no contest, was there? His friend had to agree, though he did say several times that we were talkin' about tits here and you had to go and throw in faces. After about half an hour of this, they got up and went home, each in a different direction, each calling goodnights to each other in the chilly darkness.

Karl Tolan got home around ten o'clock.

He weaved a little, indicating he'd been drinking. He went up the front steps and disappeared inside.

The voices erupted shortly thereafter. Mrs. Chambers was screaming at him. Prine couldn't hear the words, but he could pretty well imagine them. *Lawman was here askin' about you, but I got a pretty good idea what you're wanted for. Rape and murder. And I ain't about to have no rapist or murderer under my roof, you can bet on that.*

A few shouts from other boarders. *Shut up! Tryin' to sleep!*

Followed by one of those silences that are angrier than any words could be. Feet stomping up the second-floor stairs — presumably Karl Tolan — a door banging shut. Presumably him going into his room and packing things up. No shouts from the boarders for obvious reasons. Karl Tolan was nobody to rile.

Footsteps stomping down the stairs. Mrs. Chambers's last self-righteous statement: "Ain't safe no more for decent people! Not even in their own homes!"

Shrill in the night.

31

And then Karl Tolan appeared, tromping off toward town. If he was drunk when he got home tonight, the argument must have sobered him up. He wasn't drunk now. He was mightily pissed off. He swung a swollen carpetbag as he stomped along.

Prine dropped down from the tree and followed Tolan back to town.

The man took a room in The Majestic, a remnant of the boom days when even a prison cell of a room brought a formidable rent for the owner. The place was so vile that a couple of town council members had tried to have it torn down.

Prine waited a half hour across the street. Then he went home, to bed.

Chapter Four

Next morning, after a quick and early breakfast at The Friendly Café, Prine rode out to the Neville spread where Cassie and Richard Neville lived and oversaw their beef empire. An idea had come to him, a plan really. Maybe making the acquaintance of a rich woman — and a damned fine-looking one at that — wasn't out of the question at all.

He tugged his horse into a copse of birches about a quarter mile from the entrance to the ranch. Even from here, he could see the house. Hard to miss. It was built of native stone and wood, with three long wings off the central house. It reminded Prine more of an institutional building than a home. It was compelling, but coldly so. Even the shade trees around it had been planted with military precision, so that you were more impressed by the landscaping than the trees themselves.

Prine had brought his field glasses this morning. He had no trouble spotting the man who rode past him and pulled his horse into a copse of jackpines not far from Prine.

This man wore a derby and a nice suit and looked like a businessman. But as soon as he pulled his railroad watch out, checking the time, and then the small notebook from his back pocket, Prine realized that the man was working the same thing Karl Tolan was.

Twenty minutes later, Cassie appeared in his fringed buggy, heading for town. She was the prettiest sight on a morning of pretty sights.

The man gave her a ten-minute head start and then directed his horse out from behind the jackpines and started back to town himself. Prine, in turn, gave the man the same amount of head start and then he, too, took off to town.

Prine did his work. He had a court appearance, he had some possible minor rustling he checked out, and he had some paperwork to catch up on.

He spent the last hour of the day going through three stacks of old Wanted posters. Some of them were long out of date. These he pitched. A few of the posters made him smile. The descriptions of the wanted men sounded like dime novels. "Maybe the fiercest man to draw breath since Billy the Kid." Since the man was described as fifty-three years old with one blind eye and a bum leg, Prine had his doubts.

He came upon a poster for Karl Tolan just before quitting time.

He was wanted on two charges of fraud. Several posters later, Prine found the man he'd seen following Cassie Neville this morning. Ted Rooney. Same charges as the Tolan character. Fraud. Not too difficult how the division of labor went with these two. Tolan the brawn, Rooney the brains. He was surprised their legal charges weren't more severe. But all that meant was that they hadn't been caught for other and more serious crimes.

He was already getting a sense of what they were likely up to. He was surprised, in fact, that it hadn't been tried before.

He folded the posters neatly and put them in his back pocket.

That night, he sat alone at a table in a saloon, drinking slow beers and sketching out quick ideas of how the thing would actually come off.

Kidnapping had become one of the staple crimes in the New West, as the editorial writers now liked to call their frontier states. There was risk involved, of course, but from the criminal's point of view, the odds were in their favor.

You take a kid and make damned sure he or she is treated well in your custody, then send a note to the robber baron or would-be robber baron detailing just how much money you want and where you want it placed. You say that if these things are done right, the kid will be dropped off at so-and-so a place at such-and-such a time.

Now, for sure the local law will want to try and grab you, but in most cases the parents will say no, let's pay them. They look at you like these vile wild animals capable of anything. You try and cheat on them, they know damned well you'll kill their child. You think they want to be responsible for you killing their child?

That's where this kind of operation really falls down. Doing something to the kid — that is, killing, accidentally or on purpose, him or her. If the kid gets returned sound of mind and limb, they'll come after you, but only with measured zeal. You kill the kid, they'll spend every cent they have hiring bounty hunters and assassins to hunt you down. Mexico? Canada? No matter. Plenty of lean and hungry bounty hunters and assassins there, too. If you want to live on this continent, they're going to find you. One New York millionaire sent a pair of killers to France to find the murderers of his small daughter. The avengers did as they were told. They castrated the murderers, poured oil on the open wounds, and then set them on fire.

All the same rules would apply to twenty-two-year-old young women, too. Keep her safe. Return her in good fettle. And, in this case, resist the temptation to rape her. They won't come after you quite as hard for rape as they will for murder. But they'll still come after you.

Karl Tolan didn't necessarily look bright enough to know all these things — subtle wasn't a word that came to mind when you looked upon the angry, busted visage of Karl Tolan — but his partner Rooney gave the impression of being bright and competent.

Prine had three beers in all. He went home and slept well, feeling rested and ready when the rooster announced the day.

Karl Tolan said, "I just want to get it over with."

Rooney said, "That's your trouble, Karl, you always just want to get it over with."

He smiled. "I sure hope you're not like that with the ladies. They appreciate a man who takes his time."

The Skillet was a café next to the railroad roundhouse. They usually met there a couple times a day.

Tolan frowned. Always with the little digs, Rooney. If Rooney wasn't insulting him about his looks, his clothes, his body odor, his lack of education, he was reminding him that Tolan wouldn't ever make a dime without Rooney to guide him.

"I take my time, my women got no complaints," Tolan said.

"That one you gave a black eye had a few complaints, as I recall," Rooney said with a wink in his voice. "What'd you use on her, a club?"

"She called me a name."

"What name?"

"You know. A dumb bastard. Bitch."

"You went a little overboard, my friend. She could've preferred charges. And if she'd done that, Sheriff Daly would've taken a real serious interest in you. And then he might have been able to figure out what we were doing here."

"You would've hit her, too, Mac."

"No, I wouldn't've, Karl. I know how to

control myself. Like that time near Cheyenne when you went all crazy on me. If I hadn't kept myself under control, you would've gotten us both hanged." Rooney had paid the woman two hundred dollars not to turn Karl in. Karl had never even said thank you.

Six kidnappings in three years. Each successful. But the fourth one, the nine-year-old boy in the closet of the tiny house they were renting, a deputy came to the door and Karl grabbed his rifle and was about to start pumping bullets through the wood.

Thank God Rooney had been smart enough and fast enough to prevent their undoing. He grabbed the barrel of the gun and yanked the rifle from Karl. Then he whispered for Karl to go over and sit down and shut up. Karl could see how pissed Rooney was. He decided he'd better do exactly as Mac said. He went over and sat down. Mac answered the door. The boyish deputies had some questions about their next door neighbors' son. A couple people on the block said the kid was a regular hellion. Had Rooney found that to be the case? No, sir, I haven't. Few times I've seen him, he's been very polite and well-behaved. Well, thank you, sir, appreciate your time.

Nice little palaver with a hayseed deputy. Harmless as all hell.

Where dumb frantic Karl would've been blasting the shit out of the deputy through the door for no good reason at all.

"I'd like to get out of this town. Place spooks me. Why can't we do it tomorrow?" Tolan said.

"We can do it tomorrow. We can do it anytime we want. But there's one trouble."

"What's that?"

Rooney gave him his best arrogant smile. "Think real hard, Karl. I think you can figure it out for yourself."

Prine counted six cockroaches and numerous rat droppings, and found evidence of lice. This was when he'd been in Tolan's room for less than two minutes.

The room was less than the size of a jail cell. The bedclothes on the cot had so many different colors of stains on them, it resembled a Navajo rug. The air was rancid with the perpetual odors of chamber pot, cigarettes, vomit, assorted illnesses, and terrible food. But how could you gag down food in a room that smelled like this? Eating next to a latrine would be easier.

There was no bureau, no closet. Tolan's earthly goods were all packed into a grimy

40

carpetbag, which Prine dumped out on the cot.

Two shirts, one pair of trousers, three pairs of gray socks that had once been white, long johns that not even bleach could help, a comb, a jacket, a cap, a hand mirror, a Bowie knife, and six photographs of buxom naked ladies flaunting their privates.

Not a whole hell of a lot of help.

Prine was in the room for less than four minutes. He went down the same back-end fire escape he'd used to come up.

Cassie Neville said, "It's very nice to meet you, Deputy."

She gave a little curtsy that was cute as all hell. *She* was cute as all hell. Refined yet not formal at all. A girly girl who'd nonetheless probably been something of a tomboy when she'd been growing up. Today she wore a white blouse, a dark riding skirt, and a smile that could break a thousand hearts from half a mile away.

The church basement where the poor and the unemployed came for food and medicine had been painted white to give it a clean, open feeling. The doors were left open to let sunshine beam down the steps. And the other woman who helped Cassie

41

was as resolutely cheerful as she was.

Prine wanted her to remember him when she got herself kidnapped. After all, he was going to be her savior. Her hero. There would be a sizable reward offered for her return. And that sizable reward would be plenty for a man to head to California and find a place for himself in the sun and the ocean.

Prine said, "This is sure a nice thing you do. This setup for poor people, I mean."

She smiled. "They're poor in money, perhaps, Mr. Prine. But not poor in spirit. Some of the nicest, most decent people I've ever met I met right here in this church basement. Isn't that right, Effie?"

Her assistant, another daughter of wealth, nodded enthusiastic agreement. "I just wish some of my rich friends had the spirit of these people. You never hear them complain about anything."

The portrait she painted was sentimental and untrue, of course. Poor people complained all the time. As did everybody else, no matter where they stood on the social ladder. Though he was generally optimistic about things, his years as a lawman had taught Prine that when you came right down to it, life wasn't easy for anybody. There was always dire surprise, unexpected illness, family or friends in some kind of trouble, and fear that whatever you possessed — whether it was a lot or a little — would be snatched from you by the dark and comic gods who sometimes seemed in control of this vale of tears. Money solved many problems, but not all of them.

Prine scanned the basement. Against one wall were racks of clothes. Against another, stacks and stacks of canned food. Against a third wall were things for the home, everything from washboards to butter churns. Everything but the canned goods were used, but some of it looked as if it had been used only slightly.

There was a collection box. FOR THE POOR, it read. Prine took several greenbacks from his pocket and dropped them in the box.

"That's very generous of you," she said. "We really appreciate it."

"I'll try and give you a little something on a regular basis."

She reached across the front counter and touched his arm. The gesture was as intimate as a kiss. Just something about it. Just something about her warm brown eyes as she did it. "Do you enjoy piano music, Mr. Prine?"

"Very much."

"I should say classical piano music."

"The times I've heard it, I've enjoyed it very much. Not that I know much about it."

"I don't know much about it myself. But there's this neighbor of ours — a Mrs. Drummond, her husband is one of the Denver Drummonds — and she was trained musically in the East at two very good schools. She's playing at our house tonight for invited guests. Would you enjoy something like that?"

"I'd enjoy that very much."

"Why don't you stop out around seven? Would that be all right?"

Prine had been scrupulous about not fixing his gaze upon the hypnotic swell of her breasts or the beautifully proportioned curve of her hips. But just for a heady moment, his glance fell to them. And when he looked up, he found her smiling at him in that secret way of females who appreciate being admired if the admiration is discreet and courteous.

A group of Mexican women and children clattered down the steps, ending the perfect moment of romance and proper lust Prine was feeling.

"Good afternoon, Mrs. Suarez," Cassie said to the woman who reached the basement floor first.

44

"Well, I'd best get back to work," Prine said.

"I think you'll enjoy yourself tonight, Mr. Prine."

Prine smiled. "I know I will."

Every other day, Lucy gathered up all the day-old bread in a basket and took it over to the church basement, where it was given free to the poor.

Lately, on most such trips, she had to argue herself out of walking past the sheriff's office. Seeing Tom Prine was exquisite agony. She loved him too much to simply accept him as another person.

Today she was stern with herself. More than half the time, she ended up walking past the sheriff's office and then slowing down in case Tom just happened to be coming out the door.

She'd never managed to see him on one of these furtive trips.

Today, she avoided anxiety and embarrassment by walking along the river. It was a longer route, but the day was pretty and she wouldn't have to worry about Tom.

But even on this route there was a surprise for her. A handsome — almost pretty — young man sat on a stool before an easel painting the river scene he saw before him

— a crude barge and a couple of rowboats. The far shore is what would give the painting its romance. White birches and an old icehouse sat there, suggesting a gentler time when life wasn't as fast as it was now.

When he saw her, he jumped up so quickly he nearly knocked over the easel. He wore, as usual, a high-collared white shirt and tight black trousers and a gray vest. His dark curly hair lent him the air he wanted — that of an artist. His name was David Hearn, and he had been to London and Paris and Berlin before returning to his hometown of Claybank. He hadn't returned by choice. He'd never been a strong man, and a bout with consumption had left him even weaker. And it was probably just as well for him to come home. It was obvious to everybody but the blind that he didn't have much artistic talent. Even by local standards, his paintings lacked any kind of originality or even spirit. They simply recorded, with no inspiration whatsoever, what he chose to paint. His family had money and supported him in his illusions about someday being a great painter.

"You're as beautiful as an apparition, Lucy, you really are."

She laughed. "And you're as corny as a bad actor."

He rushed over to her and kissed her on the cheek. "I count it a good day when I'm able to tell you that I love you. In person, I mean. Not in one of my little drawings."

He mailed her drawings two or three times a week. With sentimental poems attached. Every once in a while they'd be funny poems. She preferred those.

"So I think you should reconsider and marry me. Think of the children we'd have. So smart and good-looking and talented —"

Merry as he was, she was well aware of the underlying sadness in his eyes and words. He really did love her — had loved her since they'd shared a one-room schoolhouse — and she sensed that he would always love her.

She was crushing him just as Tom Prine was crushing her. And like Tom, she was careful to neither encourage nor hurt David unduly.

"David —"

"There's a choir at the church tonight. You like choir music, I know you do."

"Yes, but —"

"But what? Don't tell me about Tom. I know you think he's being nice to you, but he's going on with his life."

She'd never heard malice in David's

voice before. It chilled her. She sensed now that he knew something — something she would find terrible. He'd never had any power over her, but he had some now.

"You mean he's seeing somebody?"

David put his hand to his head. "Oh, God, Lucy, forgive me. I shouldn't have brought it up. I'm so sorry."

But she was angry and not willing to give in to his sudden remorse. "You started to tell me something, David. Now you'd better damned well finish it."

He'd done serious damage to their relationship, and he knew it. He looked pale, sick, even more so than usual. "God, why did I say that?"

"I'm in a hurry, David. I have to drop this bread off at the church basement and then get right back to work."

He seemed to notice the basket of bread for the first time. He laughed sadly. "That's funny."

"What is?"

"You going to the church basement."

"Why is that funny?"

"Because that's what I was going to tell you. My mother had me drop some old clothes off there a while ago and —" He hesitated. "Damn, Lucy, I shouldn't have said anything."

"Well, you'd better say it now."

He sighed. His dramatics irritated her. "While I was there, I heard Cassie Neville invite Tom out to her house tonight. A piano recital."

"And he accepted?"

He nodded silently.

She said nothing, just began walking again toward the church.

"Lucy, Lucy, listen —" he called after her. But she paid no attention.

Her mind was filled with small dramas of how it would be when she faced Cassie, so beautiful, so elegant, so wealthy Cassie. She couldn't blame Tom for being attracted to her. At least he had good taste.

She imagined her and Cassie in an argument. Lucy declaring her love for Tom. Cassie declaring her love for Tom. The customers shocked and embarrassed at the two young women carrying on this way in public.

But when she got there, the basement was crowded. She set the basket of bread on the far counter and left. Cassie was so occupied checking people out that she didn't even notice Lucy.

Midafternoon, Rooney and Tolan rode out to the deserted farmhouse where they

49

planned to keep Cassie Neville. The place was ideal because it had a trapdoor that led to a root cellar.

As they rode, a strange melancholy came over Rooney.

Here he was, perfectly capable of killing Tolan — which he planned to do as soon as they got the ransom money — but at the same time he was also capable of knowing that in some stupid way he'd miss him. Tolan was like having a pet, a big shabby dog that you couldn't train very well but who, if you applied enough pressure, would do your bidding more often than not. Brains and brawn, as the saying went, that was the two of them.

Too much brawn, as these things went. Tolan became more and more mercurial as the years went on. Rooney suspected that all the drunken brawls he'd been in had caused some permanent damage to Tolan's senses. He was too much of a risk these days. Rooney needed somebody younger, smarter, steadier as a partner.

But still and all, he would miss old Tolan. There was no doubt about that.

As they rode out to the farmhouse, Tolan kept glancing at his partner Rooney. The man always seemed to wear that ironic, superior smile. No matter what Tolan did or said, Rooney managed to convey his superiority nearly every time.

This was one road that had run out for Tolan. There would be enough cash in this kidnapping to set him up for a good long time. One of his prison friends had a little shack down in the bayous of Louisiana and between screwing colored girls and fishing all day, the life there seemed unmatched by any other place on earth. And with the stash of greenbacks Tolan would be bringing along, he'd have money for the rest of his life — if, that is, he kept it hidden from his prison friend, who, when you faced facts, you had to admit would kill your mother for a dollar. Tolan'd have to hide his stash real, real good down there or his prison friend would kill him for it. Or maybe — it was nice to think so — all that screwing of colored girls and all that fishing had changed his prison friend. Maybe he was now a trustworthy fella. But then Tolan had never known a trustworthy fella. Or trustworthy gal, for that matter.

Tolan found himself hypnotically gazing upon Rooney's neck. He wanted there to be a lot of pain and panic and dread and total terror. Cutting a man's throat was about the best way Tolan could think of. His fingers ached for that time to arrive.

Sheriff Wyn Daly said, "You noticed anything different about Tom these last few days?"

Deputy Bob Carlyle finished up with some forms he'd been filling out on his desk and looked up. "Prine?" He considered Prine a moment. "Yeah, I guess I sort of have."

"I had to tell him three times to ride out and see the Washburn widow about somebody tearin' down that fence of hers. That isn't like him. Then he had a couple of mysterious disappearances."

Carlyle grinned. "Mysterious disappearances? Now, that sounds serious."

Every once in a while, Daly would come up with a phrase straight from a stage melodrama. Carlyle and Prine liked to ride him about it.

"You know what I mean. He'd be gone three, four hours and when he'd come back he wouldn't have any good explanation for where he'd been."

"That doesn't sound like Prine."

"No, it doesn't. That's why I'm wondering if something's wrong with him. In his life, I mean."

Carlyle dropped his pen on the desk, sat

back, and locked his hands behind his head. "I'm not bein' funny when I say this — he don't have enough of a life for somethin' to *be* wrong. Far as I know, he doesn't have a woman or any kin. Told me his folks died some time ago."

"That's what he told me, too."

"He was seein' that Lucy over at the café, but I think she scared him off. Always talkin' about marriage and such."

Daly stuck his unlit briar in his mouth. "He seem to be havin' a hard time with anything he's workin' on?"

"Not that he's mentioned to me. I meant what I said the other day. He's a damned good deputy. A hell of a lot better with people than I am, for one thing. And he keeps that desk of his organized twenty-four hours a day. Not like this piece of shit." Carlyle's desk was a paper swamp of forms, letters, legal documents, and arrest sheets he wrote out every time he brought somebody in.

"Maybe there's a gal he hasn't told us about," Daly said.

"Could be."

"Or maybe he's just not feelin' well."

"There's somethin' goin' around, that's for sure. Two of my little granddaughters got sore throats."

Daly glanced back at his own desk. It wasn't exactly a monument to orderliness either.

Prine came in an hour later carrying a package from the general store. He set it over in the corner of the office and sat down at his desk.

Both Daly and Carlyle were busy doing paperwork.

Prine opened the middle drawer of his desk, where he kept work that he had yet to complete. When he looked over at the other two, he realized they were watching him. Carefully. He wondered what the hell was going on.

"You get to Liddy Washburn yet?" Daly said.

"Thought I'd do that soon as I finish up with these two forms. I've got to get them over to the post office."

"Damned forms," Carlyle said. "I'd like to burn every one of them."

"You must've been pretty busy this afternoon, not getting around to Liddy yet," Daly said.

"Yeah, I was busy," Prine said. And then he turned back to his work before Daly could ask anything else.

Prine finished up his two forms, stuck

54

them in appropriate envelopes, slapped stamps on them, and then said, "Well, I'll head out to Washburn's place now."

Daly smiled. "I knew he wouldn't do it. Didn't you, Bob?"

"No, to tell you the truth. I figured he *would* do it."

"You two ever going to tell me what the hell you're talking about?"

Daly winked at Carlyle. "Listen to this, will you. Like he don't know what we're talkin' about."

"I really don't." Prine felt the way he had when he was a little kid and his older brothers kept the ball from him, throwing it back and forth over his head so he couldn't catch it.

"The sack," Daly said. "Carlyle here wrote me a note while you were busy working on your forms. He said you'd tell us what was in the sack before you left."

Prine felt his cheeks heat up. "Hell, can't I have any personal business?"

"Sure, you can, son. We're just trying to figure out why you're acting the way you are the last few days," Daly said.

"And just how would that be, Sheriff? I'm acting the way I usually do."

"Not really," Carlyle said. "You're just — different is all."

55

"We worry about you, Tom. We like you. We want to make sure that everything is all right."

"And why wouldn't everything be all right?" Prine said.

"We don't know," Carlyle said. "That's what we hope you'd tell *us*."

"Well, if there is anything wrong, the answer sure isn't in that bag over there."

"Why don't you let us judge that for ourselves?" Daly said, smiling. He obviously sensed he was making Prine nervous, which meant that there was something revealing in the bag, after all.

Prine went over and picked up the sack and said, "You're so eager to get me out to the Washburn place, I'd better get going."

Carlyle laughed. "Boy, that must be somethin' in that sack."

"Something," Daly said, "mighty special. Just look at him blush."

Prine shook his head. "You're like two little kids. Little devils."

"We got him now, Sheriff."

"I think you're right. I think we got him real good."

Prine scoffed and then tossed the bag so that it landed on the sheriff's desk. "There. Go ahead and look. Look till your eyes fall out."

But Daly wasn't done teasing. "You know, Bob, I almost don't want to open it."

"Now, why would that be, Sheriff?"

"Well, when a fella builds somethin' up as much as Prine here did — well, you're just bound to be disappointed when you finally see what it is."

"You could be right about that, Sheriff," Carlyle said, going along with the sly tone.

"You idiots," Prine said.

He walked to Daly's desk, grabbed the sack, shoved his hand inside, and brought forth a handsome, expensive black western shirt with the kind of white piping they wear in Wild West shows. About as fancy as a feller could get in a burg like Claybank.

"You got matchin' silver pistols to go with this shirt?" Daly said.

"Very funny," Prine said. "Now, if you're finally satisfied, I'll take my shirt and ride on out to the Washburn place."

"Be sure and wear your shirt," Carlyle said. "I hear those widow women get awful lonely. And she sees you in that shirt, she's liable to come runnin' out to greet you bare naked."

Daly smirked. "She's got a nice set on her, nobody could argue with that."

Prine decided to have a little fun on his terms. He said, "I'm more worried what Cassie Neville thinks of me than the widow Washburn."

"Cassie Neville? You spendin' time with her?" Carlyle said. "Oh, bullshit."

"Afraid it's not," Prine said.

"You serious, Tom?"

"Invited me out to her place tonight. Some kind of violin recital. Some girl who studied music back east."

"Well, I'll be damned," Carlyle said. "He ain't woofin'."

"Cassie Neville?" Daly said. "No offense, Tom, but I thought she . . ."

"Well, she apparently changed her mind," Prine said. "At least for a night."

There was no doubting the pleasure in his voice. Not only had Cassie Neville actually invited him to her mansion, Prine had also had the extreme fun of seeing Daly and Carlyle stammer and stutter and try to make some sense of how — even if he was young, strong, and nice-looking — a deputy got himself an invite to such an event.

"Well, gentlemen, I guess I'd better get out to the Washburn place."

He turned when he got to the door, his sack under his arm, and gave them the big-

58

gest grin he could summon. "And I sure wouldn't want to hold my new friend Cassie up, either."

Both men gaped. Neither said a single word.

CHAPTER FIVE

The horseshoe-shaped drive in front of the plantation-style house allowed room for every expensive, elegant, and remarkable surrey and buggy in the area. Three Mexican servants in red coats, white shirts, and black trousers hastened about helping people with their vehicles, then leading them to the open front doors of the mansion.

Conversation and laughter poured from the doors. Many of the guests had arrived somewhat early and the liquor was flowing freely. Richard Neville was a drinker, even if his sister was not.

Some of the younger guests strolled the perfectly kept rolling lawns on the sides and back end of the house. They were dressed so well they looked, from a distance, like huge flowers in the gauzy half-moon dusk, lilies floating on a stream perhaps.

Prine's first reaction to all this — he was the only person to arrive on horseback — was to flee. He'd grown up poor enough to be intimidated by anybody who seemed connected. He knew that a lot of rich people were stupid, venal, and corrupt — probably just about the same percentage of poor people who were that way — but they had a social edge he couldn't deny. And in the face of them, he always stammered and made foolish statements. As soon as he left the party tonight, he'd think of all the dumb and inappropriate and shitkicker things he'd said. He could get drunk, of course, but that would ensure that his remarks would be even dumber.

He stood just inside the doors, in a vestibule large enough to hold twenty people. The servants didn't seem to know quite how to deal with him. True, he wore his nice new shirt, but all the other men wore suits and cravats.

Finally, Cassie swept up in a navy blue chiffon gown that hinted at cleavage and exposed a span of elegant, fragile shoulder.

"You certainly look handsome tonight."

He gulped, hoping that nobody nearby had heard her. He wasn't good at accepting compliments in public. "You sure look pretty yourself."

She leaned to his ear to whisper. "Don't worry about being shy. I'm the same way. But my brother needs me to play hostess, so I have to force myself to be outgoing."

She touched his hand. Pleasure flooded him. He hadn't felt like this in a long, long time. "C'mon, I'll introduce you to Richard. I've told him all about you."

"I didn't think you knew that much about me."

"Oh, I'm a devil, Tom. I have spies everywhere."

Her perfume was hypnotic. He followed her through the mansion.

The home managed to feel spacious despite the fact that each room he glimpsed was filled with art and artifacts of all kinds. He didn't know what periods the various furnishings came from, only that the furnishings had been organized to complement the art. One room was given over to French art. He recognized it because he'd happened to see an article about it. The furnishings were all French, too, including a large fireplace whose mantel was covered with a line of music boxes that two women were discussing. The tiny sounds were quaint and fetching in the large room. The paintings were all of girls in ballet poses. He could imagine Cassie in such attire and pose.

The flooring was parquet, the decorative molding and trim on the walls classically Roman. In the halls, huge urns of numerous colors gleamed in the dancing light of carefully placed sconces. Two of the large rooms he saw had verandas off them, crowded verandas. People were everywhere, perhaps a hundred in all.

The music room was large enough to seat everybody. A grand piano sat near open French doors that let in a slash of dramatic moonlight. A rather square-bodied young girl with thick eyeglasses and a moon face and a pink formal sat at the piano, not playing, simply staring, as if she were having a secret dialogue with it. Prine felt sorry for her. He would have preferred — as would most of the people here — that she were a slip of a girl whose ethereal face hinted at a charming and socially acceptable form of eroticism. He felt guilty for not being able to accept her as she was. What the hell, why couldn't a sort of mannish girl play a good piano?

He'd seen Richard Neville around town many times, so he recognized him right away — the handsome, blond man whose size and power made him the focus of any room he walked into. There were men like that. You could say it was their money, you could say it was their looks, you could say it was their cunning. But what you really meant was that there were men — and women — whose magnetism would have been just as strong without any of these things. They were the superior branch of the species, and there was no denying it.

Neville, like most superior people, was holding court. He talked, you listened. This particular portion of his godlike utterances had to do with a short-haul railroad he was thinking of investing in — and that he wanted them to invest in, too.

They waited at the edges of the court until Richard released his charges. "But you didn't come here to listen to me," he said with no hint of modesty in his voice — of *course* you came here to listen to me! — "you came here to have fun."

And then Neville came forward like a politician sighting a particularly scruffy poor person. "Hello there," he said, pushing forth a wealth of hand that was twice the size of Prine's. At least he didn't try to impress Prine with his strength. Strapping blond gods didn't need to impress people. People knew enough to be impressed without having a demonstration. "You're Prine. You work for Sheriff Daly. Darned good man. I got him elected the first time, and I'll keep right on getting him reelected. And you can tell him that for me. I think he's done a fine job."

He looked around to see if any of his courtesans were nodding in agreement, but, to his surprise, they seemed to have found other interests.

"And my sweet little sister has told me a lot of good things about you, too," he went on. "I'm not always too happy with her choice of friends. Her taste will improve as she grows up and learns to be responsible. But from everything I've heard, you're a start in the right direction, Prine. And I'm darned happy you could be here tonight. Now, if you'll excuse me . . ."

Prine wondered how old Neville had been when he adopted this act. The insolence in his eyes had been expressed only once, in the dismissive, nasty way he'd referred to his sister. Otherwise the act had been without fault. Hail-fellow-well-met and all that businessman bullshit. But Prine knew better. What you had in Richard Neville was an animal who could go dangerous on you in a second. No wonder he'd tripled the value of his father's estate. No wonder he was being talked about as the next governor.

A man Prine didn't know, a man who was probably drunker than he should have been at a recital, bumped into Prine and nearly sloshed his drink all over Prine's sleeve.

"Whatever you do," the man said, overenunciating as drunks do, "don't ever borrow any money from him. He'll never let you hear the end of it. Especially when things're going bad. He just keeps right on you anyway. Like you could help it that things're going bad." The man waggled a finger in Prine's face. "Don't borrow money from him, you hear me?"

Prine smiled. "You've got my word on it."

The man's head rotated as if it were on ball bearings. "And don't you forget it."

The recital was an ordeal.

Before each endless number, the girl would pronounce the name of the composer in very bad halting French — at least Prine *assumed* it was bad French; for all he knew it might be bad Italian — and then proceed to play the piece. Even Prine could tell she was making a lot of mistakes. He felt sorry for her again. But he also felt sorry for himself. This wasn't his sort of an evening. A couple of beers, a couple of sentimental songs on the player piano in some latrine of a saloon — that was the sort of recital he was used to.

Apparently, he wasn't radiating any of his boredom. He sat next to Cassie. She kept squeezing his hand. And smiling. And breaking his heart. He was stricken with her, positively stricken.

There was an intermission. Everybody raving *how wonderful how wonderful* to the pianist's parents and then obviously loading up on liquor so they could get through the second half of the recital.

Cassie excused herself for a few minutes. Prine walked around the mansion. He couldn't see how anybody could live here. It was like visiting some vast institution, like the museum or library in Denver.

He nodded to people, but he was quick to steer clear of conversations. He didn't want to toss and turn all night, thinking of the stupid things he'd said. Better to say nothing at all.

He recognized the voice long before he saw it. He'd taken a westward turn somewhere near the back of the house. A servant passed by a closed door, shaking his head at the loud voice. The servant glanced at Prine, frowned, and hurried away.

The voice belonged to Richard Neville.

"The champagne is flat. The beef is tough. And the crepes are all but inedible.

Dammit, Cassie, can't I put you in charge of anything? My God, when are you going to grow up?"

Prine had partaken of the champagne, the beef, and the crepes and found them to be pretty damned good. Of course, he was a sixty-dollar-a-month deputy. He was not one of the great gods stalking the earth.

Neville settled down finally. "Next time, please do a better job. That's all I ask. That you apply yourself. Apply yourself, Cassie." He sounded like the teacher all the kids hated. There was a prissy, prim side to his superiority.

"I did everything I could, Richard. I honestly did. Everything came from Denver. And everybody else seems to like it. They've been complimenting me on it all night."

He laughed harshly. "God, you're so naive sometimes, Cassie. What else would they say? That it's tripe? That they're insulted that a family of our standing would offer things like this? Of course not. Polite people don't hurt other people's feelings."

"You don't seem to mind hurting mine, Richard." She'd found a little bit of anger and dignity. Prine hoped she'd build on it.

"I'm doing this for your sake, Cassie. You never seem to take that into account.

I'm doing this for your sake. If I didn't love you, I wouldn't spend so much time trying to turn you into a mature and responsible young woman. And while we're at it —"

"Don't say a word against Tom Prine," she snapped.

"I'm sure he's a nice young man," he said. "But my Lord, Cassie, a deputy? What kind of a job is that? You need someone with a future, someone like —"

"Like you, Richard?"

Her remark apparently hurt him. "Am I that bad, Cassie? I've raised you, don't forget. Dad didn't. Dad was always too busy. So I took the time and trouble to make sure that you were growing up the right way. And look at how you treat me now."

Another pose, guise. The deeply hurt saint. All I've done for you; all I've sacrificed for you.

And she went for it.

A rustle of evening gown; Cassie sighing. "I'm sorry, Richard. I never should've said that. And I really will do better next time. I promise."

Tell him he's a pompous shit, Prine thought. Don't take the blame. Tell him where to put it.

"Next time I'll let you know every store

I'm buying from before I place the orders. Won't that be better, Richard?"

"That'll be much better, Cassie."

Easy to picture her, so slight, in her brother's arms. Playing guilty child to his stern pastor.

"You'll grow up yet," he said, "and be a mature woman who finds herself a worthy husband. You wait and see."

Prine hurried back to the music room.

When the recital was over and the gushing begun, Cassie took Prine's arm and guided him out to one of the verandas.

The night was warm for autumn. The moon had that fierce ancient aspect that the Aztecs built so much of their religion on. Dark gods hidden in the pocked fierce silver face.

Her earlier cheerfulness was gone. Obviously, Richard berating her had taken its toll. She was still unhappy.

She leaned against the hip-high stone wall and said, "You know something stupid about me?"

"Hard to believe *anything* stupid about you."

He leaned against the wall next to her. She touched his arm again.

"I still read children's books."

"What's wrong with that?"

"Richard thinks I'm immature. Silly, actually. He thinks I'm silly. And that just proves it, I suppose."

"Richard isn't always right."

She laughed, but there was nothing gay about it. "He gives that impression, doesn't he? He's always been like that. My father was like that. But Richard is twice as bad. Three times. But you know something, if I ever had nerve enough to tell him that, he'd deny it. I don't think he's aware of it."

"Maybe," Prine said.

She leaned forward slightly so she could see his face. "You didn't like him, did you?"

"I was taking a tour of the house. I heard him arguing with you. Nobody should talk to you that way."

She covered her face with her hands, the way a small, embarrassed girl would. Then she surprised him by laughing. This time the sound was merry. Her hands came down.

"It must've sounded terrible."

"The worst part was that you didn't fight back. You started to. But then you stopped."

"He scares me, Tom. I could never stand up to him."

"Everything was fine tonight. I heard people say that over and over. And you weren't around, so they weren't just flattering you. Everything was fine for everybody but your brother."

She leaned back again. They were silent for a time. The sounds of the party floated out the veranda door. A lot of social gush from the women; a lot of political guff from the men. The women wondered who'd have the best Christmas party; the men wondered if now would be a good time for Richard Neville to announce for governor.

Cassie said, "I suppose it's because he had to be the man of the house. Richard, I mean. Father was gone a lot. Mom depended on him, and so did I. I suppose that gave him a certain arrogance. Here was this very wealthy young man — not much more than a boy, really — and he spoke with the authority of my father's estate."

"Doesn't matter," Prine said. "He still doesn't have any right to treat you that way."

One of the servants came to the edge of the veranda and asked if Cassie could come to the kitchen for a moment.

"I really need to do this, Tom. I'll be back as soon as I can."

"It's all right, I need to go anyway. I need to get up early tomorrow."

She kissed him. It was a quick, chaste kiss, but a kiss nonetheless. It made him feel ridiculously important.

"I hope I see you again, Tom."

He smiled, still under the spell of her kiss. "Oh, I imagine that could be arranged."

"I was afraid you might have been put off by tonight and —"

He took her hand. He wasn't good at moments like these. His tongue became heavy as a boat oar and his heart threatened to explode on him. Sex was a whole lot easier than romance.

"I had a good time."

"You liked the music?"

"I really enjoyed it."

"Isn't she wonderful?"

"She sure is."

"You're lying, aren't you?"

"Yes, I am."

She gave him a grin that stayed with him all the rest of the night. Then she gave him a fake girly punch in the stomach. He was surprised and pleased to find her that playful.

"But," he said, "I'd sit through another recital just like that one if I got to sit next to you."

She was wise enough to end on that note, a perfect romantic line.

Another kiss. Not so quick, not so chaste, and then she was gone.

On the ride back to town, all he could think of was the kidnapping. Maybe he should tell her, warn her. Much as he wanted to collect the reward and be the hero, what if something went wrong? Things often went wrong with kidnappings. But what if — ?

But no, he wouldn't let that happen. He'd rescue her right away. Before anything could go wrong.

He was sure of it.

CHAPTER SIX

When the mail came in the morning, Sheriff Daly looked through it, as usual, and then dropped an envelope on Prine's desk.

"You have room in that busy social schedule to do a little job for me this morning?"

Daly and Carlyle had been joshing Prine all morning.

"I suppose," Prine said. "Just as long as I don't have to get my hands dirty."

"A charmed life," Carlyle said.

"You won't have to get your hands dirty," Daly said, "but you'll probably wear out some shoe leather. Guy's probably off on a bender somewhere, or shacked up with a whore — or both. But we need to check it out."

Dear Sheriff Daly,

A week ago one of our freelance investigators went to Claybank to work on an arson investigation. His name is Allan Woodward, and from long experience we know him to be a sober, steady worker.

75

He ordinarily keeps us informed via telegram as to how his investigation is going. We received two telegrams from him in the first three days. But since then we've heard nothing. He told us he'd be staying at the Empire Hotel.

Would you or one of your deputies please check with the hotel and see if he's still registered there? If he's not, could you ask around town and see if anybody knows where he might be. We haven't told his wife about this. But we are concerned. Al isn't the sort to just disappear.

Sincerely,
Evan Ramsdell
Vice President
Nationwide Insurance Company

"Anybody want to bet he's on a bender?" Prine said.

"Why bet? I'd just lose." Carlyle grinned. "He probably met one of Miss Evie's gals and fell in love."

"Miss Evie keeps telling me she and her gals are 'harmless,'" Daly said. "But every once in a while one of her gals ruins a marriage."

"In the arms of love," Prine smiled,

quoting the beginning of a bawdy poem that was a saloon favorite.

He stood up, cinched on his hat, waved the envelope for Nationwide Insurance at the others, and walked out the door.

Karl Tolan didn't like confined spaces, so the root cellar was something he wanted to get into and out of as soon as possible.

Once he got the lantern lighted — the flame dull in the eleven a.m. light through the window — he opened the trapdoor and proceeded to climb down the ladder.

The dirt walls and floor and the subterranean chill put him in mind of a grave. What else would it put him in mind of? That's what the damned thing was, wasn't it?

A grave where you stored fruits and vegetables to keep them fresh. But a grave nonetheless.

He needed to set it up so that it was just right.

He'd already moved down an extra lantern, a chair, and a military cot for her. There was even a heavy quilt. He'd dug a small latrine, lugged down half a gallon of water plus a glass, and laid in a healthy supply of fruit and bread. When the authorities checked it out, they'd be able to see that the whole operation had been thoroughly planned and that she'd been thoroughly taken care of.

He didn't like to think of her. She was clean — physically clean — in a way that only added to the sexuality she radiated. She was the type of girl a man like him could never have. They would literally rather die than give in to somebody like him.

He tried not to think of that night in Dodge City.

Stumbling back to his hotel, drunk and angry at something he could no longer remember. Seeing the lady. Older than he liked them, forty maybe. But proper. Out trying to find her drunken husband, as things turned out.

He could not control himself. He came up behind her, got his hand across her mouth, and then dragged her into an empty sale barn. He hit her just once, hard enough to scare her into submission. My God, he could still feel that flesh. So tender. So clean. So . . . proper.

He'd ripped her clothes off in a frenzy. She had decided to lie back and simply let him have her. She spoke only once, and that was to ask him not to hit her again, that she was afraid.

He could also recall in humiliating detail

dropping down between her spread legs and feeling her juicy, hot center. And then reaching down and —

And nothing.

He had just assumed that he would be hard and ready for her. But his sex was soft, unwilling, unable, or both.

She must have sensed how he would ultimately respond to this humiliation, for she tried to help him, first with her knowing hand and then with her knowing mouth. But neither helped.

He remained — unable.

And man did he beat her then.

Beat her the way he would a man. Blamed *her*, of course. Should never have tried it with one of these snotty bitches who always put on such airs around men like him.

Beat her until her shrieks started to sober him up —

He stole the first saddled horse he could find and rode away from Dodge City. You do what he'd done to a proper woman like that, they'd put you in prison for a long, long time. In the wrong town they'd lynch you, even though you hadn't killed her.

He had no money. He had a Colt. That was it.

He went all the way to Montana on a

succession of stolen horses and meals in churches where they fed the poor.

He ended up in Butte, which was where he met up with Mac Rooney, which had been his hope. Rooney had never run a scam in Butte. He considered it his "safe" town, where the law regarded him as a good citizen.

Tolan had tried to live on his own for a year and it hadn't worked. Much as he resented Rooney, he needed to collect himself, eat well, sleep well, start making some money again. He hadn't been able to do any of these things on his own. . . .

And now he was in a grave, the cold and the smell of the cold spooking him. He had a fascination for stories about being buried alive, which were much in the news.

He did his rodent search again. He'd smashed a couple of rats with the shovel that lay near the ladder. There was a way you could get them on the head at just the right angle and their brains would explode. It was funny to see. Rooney told him to check each time he came down here. He didn't see any rats today.

He started toward the ladder, wanting to get out of here. Someday he'd be spending a long, long time in an underground place just like this one. Except it'd be a lot narrower. And there wouldn't be any ladder leading out.

"Nope, haven't seen him for three days," the desk clerk at the Empire Hotel said. He had a pencil-thin lady killer mustache, a soiled celluloid collar, and bulging blue eyes. "We've been getting sort of curious ourselves. He seems to be a reliable sort. No women up in the room. A beer or two before bedtime in the saloon over there. Very friendly to everybody. And then, all of a sudden, we just don't see him. And he isn't the type who'd skip out on a bill. I can practically guarantee you that."

"He make friends with anybody here in particular?"

"I'm not sure. I do know he was working on that Pentacle fire."

"Pentacle Mattress Company?"

"That's right. He mentioned that, and then he mentioned that he was an insurance investigator. So I figured maybe something was funny with the fire."

"Arson?"

"Don't see what else it could be, do you? Him being an insurance investigator and all." He nodded to the saloon in the hotel. Here they called it a gentleman's room. Which meant that the drunks didn't puke on the floor, they went outside; and the brawlers tried never to actually kill anybody on the premises. They took that outside, too. "Verne, he's the night man, he usually rolls in here about four o'clock in the afternoon. Verne, he could tell you a lot more about Mr. Woodward than I could."

"You got a home address for Verne?"

The desk clerk smiled. The smile was as oily as his hair. "How about you walk up those stairs over there and try Room D-2? He should be gettin' up just about now. It's an awful long way to go. But I think you can make it."

Prine thanked him for the directions but not the humor.

There were a thousand thousand Vernes in the New West. Transplanted easterners who'd come west for excitement and ended up tending bar or peddling all kinds of bullshit new products to housewives they daydreamed of humping if the husband wasn't around.

Verne Jenkins was easy to spot because of the silk robe. Only a man from the East would wear a black silk robe with little yellow dragons stitched into it. Nothing effeminate about it. Just too fancy by half was all. A last vestige of Verne Jenkins's life in the East.

He invited Prine in. One big room that was half living room, with a horsehair couch, a small bookcase, and a wooden table covered with liquor of various kinds. Framed photographs of New York covered the walls. A messed double bed took up most of the back half of the room. His closet was a piece of clothesline strung from one angle of a wall to another.

He said, "Yeah, me 'n' a couple of the regulars were talking about him just last night."

"Woodward?"

"Umm-hmm. Two nights ago, he asked directions to Stone Lake and said he'd be back in here around ten."

"He say why he was going to Stone Lake?"

"Said he had business was all. He didn't mind telling you that he was an investigator. Sometimes those boys play it pretty close to the vest."

"You ever see him with anybody else?"

"Nope. Never did. I mean, he'd talk to the regulars and me. But no, never saw him come in or leave with anybody else."

"Anybody ever ask you questions about him?"

Jenkins, a heavyset man with thinning gray hair and some kind of small birthmark on his right jaw, thought for a time and said, "No. Not that I can think of."

"How was his mood the last time you saw him?"

Jenkins shrugged. "About the same as always. Talked about his wife and kids. Talked about how he was going to put up a fence when he got home." Jenkins laughed. "He said the only enemies he had in the whole world were the damned gophers on his property."

"Anybody in your place take a dislike to him?"

"There wasn't anything to dislike, Deputy. He was a nice, steady guy. Friendly to everybody. Didn't drink too much, talk too much, or argue with anybody. I'd have to say he was just about the perfect customer."

"You remember if he was carrying anything with him before he went to Stone Lake?"

"Carrying?"

"Briefcase. Manila envelope. Anything like that."

Jenkins snapped his finger. "I nearly forgot. I got real busy serving people. He got sort of isolated down at the far end of the bar. He only had the one beer. Which was like him. He still had work to do, so he wasn't going to get all drunked up the way some people did. He told me once that when you were your own boss you had to be stricter with yourself than if you had a regular boss. Or you'd fail. And that's true. My business isn't any different. I could slough off, get in a conversation, let customers wait a long time for their drinks. But I can't. I wouldn't have any business if I did."

"You were going to tell me something you said you forgot."

Jenkins laughed again. "It's early in the morning for me. I played poker till dawn. After the saloon closed. What I forgot, anyway, was the envelope."

"He had an envelope?"

"Little one. The size you use for personal mail. Like if you were writing a sweetheart or something."

"Where did he have it?"

"Lying on the bar. Just kind of staring at it."

"He say anything about it to you?"

"Not a thing."

"Where was the envelope the last time you saw it, Mr. Jenkins?"

"He was putting it away in his pocket."

"You sure he didn't say anything to you?"

"Nothing. And I was kind've curious about it. I've got a curious nature as it is. And so when I see somebody like Woodward just staring down at this letter in real deep thought —"

"When he was staring, did he look upset?"

"Not upset exactly — thoughtful, I'd say. That's the right word, I guess. Thoughtful."

Ten minutes later, the desk clerk let Prine into Woodward's room.

Nothing untoward. Everything neat, orderly, as befitted a man everybody described as calm and orderly.

"I need to get back downstairs. If you need anything I'll be at the desk."

"Thanks."

Prine spent the first fifteen minutes going through Woodward's two carpetbags. A large number of family photos filled one bag. This was one true family man. And one who apparently dearly missed his wife and kids when he was away from them. Kids posing with a baseball bat, a jack-o'-lantern, next to a snowman, standing in their school classroom; mom, a plump and pretty woman, at various ages, roughly twenty to late thirties or so, in a variety of poses, expressions, and garments. Very few of Woodward himself. Stocky man with a somber but not unfriendly face. The eyes shrewd and intelligent. Except for maybe fifteen pounds, he didn't look much different at forty or so than he had when he was twenty.

Prine next went through two large ledger books where Woodward had notes on cases dating back two years. He was indeed in Claybank investigating possible arson at the Pentacle Mattress plant. Prine remembered the case. The local fire chief — admittedly an amateur — hadn't found anything queer about it. But Woodward was a professional. If there was something to be found, his pride and instincts and wisdom would lead him to it.

Prine wasn't exactly sure what he was reading — Woodward used a lot of technical jargon — but the parts he could understand signified that Woodward had no doubt he was dealing with arson.

Prine stayed half an hour in all. The most useful things were the notes he found relating to Pentacle. Not that he could understand most of them.

When you walked in the front door of Pentacle, you were standing about four feet from a desk where a woman whose severe black dress gave her the look of an Amish lady pounded on a typewriter.

"May I help you?" she asked.

Or tried to. Because over her words came a harsh cry and another female voice, younger, more refined, shouting, "Of course you don't worry about my family's reputation. That's because you came from a family that never had a good one."

She appeared moments later, a strawberry blond of early middle age, whose face was lush with a matronly sexuality that was endorsed by beautifully shaped breasts beneath her light blue dress.

She was crying. "I'm sorry about this, Mae," she said to the receptionist. "I shouldn't have come down here."

Mae smiled sympathetically and said, "That's quite all right, Mrs. Duncan. We all have family squabbles sometimes."

Mrs. Duncan glared at Prine as if he had no right to be here — hell, no right to exist here or anywhere else — and then hurried through the front door.

After a minute, Mae said, quietly, "Let's start over. May I help you?"

A thirtyish man Prine had seen at the recital last night said, "Please tell Mr. Woodward for me that I'm sorry I wasn't nicer to him. My wife was under the weather and I was worried about her, so when he came out here —"

This was the wife who'd just fled his office. It was the only time he mentioned her.

Aaron Duncan was the owner of Pentacle. He had the city suit, the city talk, the city disdain in the city eyes — and Prine didn't like him especially.

Duncan's office was now in the upstairs of the Claybank Trust Company. He had explained that these would be his quarters until the factory could be rebuilt.

"You saw him when, Mr. Duncan?"

"Monday morning. What a way to start a Monday, huh? Your wife is sick and some investigator is all but accusing you of arson."

"So it wasn't arson?"

The city eyes were angry, but the city mouth remained sociable. "Of course it was arson, Deputy Prine. When I was a child, that's all I ever wanted to be — an arsonist. You can ask my folks. They'll tell you. I loved fire. I burned down everything I could find. So of course I couldn't wait to burn down my own factory." He smiled with great unconcealed hatred and arrogance. "I'm not smart enough to be an arsonist. I can't pound a nail in straight. I can't fix my little boy's bicycle when the chain comes off. His mother can fix it, but I can't. I even burn myself when I light my own cigars, Deputy Prine. Now, does that sound like I'm an arsonist?"

"You could have hired it done."

"Could have, but didn't. Sorry to say it. For both you and Woodward's sake." Then he leaned forward and said, "Good Lord, it *is you*. When you walked in here last night, I thought you looked sort of familiar. You were with Cassie."

"Yes."

"Lord, if I wasn't married . . ." He didn't have to complete the thought. Prine felt an idiotic jealousy. He'd spent a brief evening with Cassie and now no one was permitted to talk about her in his presence?

"Well, I certainly wish you luck." He nodded to a clock on the wall. "Unfortunately, I'll have to cut this short. Rotary meets over lunch. We've got a speaker from Cheyenne today, talking about a Wild West show he's putting together. He's trying to raise capital, of course. He claims that this one is different. It's all Indian. Not a white man in it. Takes Indian history all the way back." He winked. It was meant to be an intimate wink — one shared by members of the masculinity club — but it came off as juvenile. "I'll tell him you get a few scantily dressed Indian girls in that show and I'll invest in a minute." He was more than happy to smile at his own wit.

He walked Prine to the door, a friendly hand on Prine's shoulder. Prine wanted to give him a quick elbow shot. Break a rib or two. He hadn't learned a damned thing, and that was just the way Duncan here wanted it.

Prine still wondered what Duncan's wife had been so upset about.

CHAPTER SEVEN

In the daylight, Stone Lake was a placid blue oval of water. The beach area was covered with small stones and two massive boulders. Hence the name. Prine spent twenty minutes walking around, looking for anything that remotely suggested Woodward's presence. He'd undoubtedly come here to meet somebody. But who? And what had that person done to him?

Prine stared at the water for some time. The center of the lake. Out where you'd dump a body you never wanted anybody to see. Sometimes these small lakes ran deep.

After the lake, he walked up to the timber. These woods would require a day's work to walk through. If Woodward had been murdered, he could well be in a shallow grave.

Prine assumed now that Woodward was dead. From what he'd learned of the man, Woodward was too reliable a person to just disappear.

But whom had he met? And why?

It was reasonable to assume that the

arson investigation was involved. It was also, therefore, logical to assume that somebody had lured Woodward here with supposed information about the arson.

And then murdered him.

Prine walked around the lake a final time. He didn't find much this time, either. Not that he had any idea what he was looking for. The killer probably hadn't left him a personal letter: *Here's where I threw the body in, Prine.*

But the lapping waters of the past few days had washed the sand clean of footprints. Plenty of evidence of animal tracks, none of human.

Not a button, not a piece of fabric, not a bullet casing.

Nada nada nada.

"I'd like you to tell me about the Pentacle fire."

"The Pentacle fire?" Sheriff Daly said. "What the hell's that got to do with anything?"

"You wanted me to find this Woodward. And that's what I've spent the day doing."

It was that lazy hour in the office right before suppertime. The business of the day was trailing off — official meetings, informal meetings, spontaneous meetings,

meetings-you-ran-from-but-that-ensnared-you-anyway — and now was the lull before all the saloon woes of the evenings. If this town was ever voted dry — as some communities had been leaning to lately — it wouldn't have needed a nighttime deputy. Everybody'd be home snug in their beds and minding their own business.

"So you found him, Tom?" Carlyle said.

"I think I found him."

"Now, that don't make a lot of sense, Tom," Daly said. "You either found him or you didn't."

"Stone Lake. I've just got this strong sense he's at the bottom of it."

"Why would he be at the bottom of Stone Lake?" Daly said.

So Prine went through what he'd learned. The suspected arson. The letter Woodward received. The inquiry he'd made about Stone Lake.

"So maybe Woodward was onto something?" Carlyle said.

"At least the killer thought he was."

"The fire chief," Daly said, "didn't see any trouble with the fire."

"I found Woodward's notes, Sheriff. He was sure it was arson."

"So if he's dead, where does that leave us, Tom?" Carlyle said.

"I suppose we could let the insurance company know what I know."

"But we don't know anything for sure," Daly said.

"All we need to say at this point is that I checked it out and that Woodward seems to be missing and that we hope he'll turn up. They'll figure the rest out for themselves."

"They'll figure out that he's dead?" Daly asked.

"The reputation he's got, they'll know he's not off somewhere with a jug and a whore. They'll know that he would have wired them if he'd been able to."

"You know," Daly said in the slow, cautious way he had when he questioned a deputy's theory, not wanting to hurt the man's feelings. "Natural causes are always a part of this. He was thrown by a horse and is lying unconscious somewhere. Or he had a heart attack and there isn't much left of him once the coyotes got hold of him. Or he decided to have one last big fling before he got his gold retirement watch and his wife picked out their burial plot."

"Natural causes, that I could see. A fling? Sheriff, you have to hear people talk about him. The guy's practically a saint — in their eyes, anyway."

"So will you telegram the insurance company for me?"

"Sure, Sheriff. I'll go and do it now, before supper."

All this time he'd been talking, he'd been sitting on the edge of Carlyle's desk. He hadn't made it over to his own desk yet.

When he got there, the first thing he saw was the letter. A soft blue envelope. His name written on the front in a round feminine style.

"Lucy left that for you," Carlyle said.

"I figured," Prine said.

"She's a fine gal," Daly said.

Prine scowled at him. "She got to you, too, huh, Sheriff? I knew she had Bob there in her rooting section. But now it's you, too, huh?"

"It's not a matter of her 'getting to me,' Tom. I just happen to think she's a very pretty, very intelligent gal who'd make you a damned good wife. Sensible and down-to-earth. Worked hard for every pittance she's ever made."

"As opposed to Cassie Neville and all her evil money and her snotty friends."

"Cassie's a very nice gal, too. For her own kind."

"Men who can afford her, in other words," Carlyle said.

"We're only saying this with your best interests in mind, Tom," Daly said.

Prine smirked. "What'd she do, promise you each a piece of free pie if you agreed to tree me for her?"

Carlyle laughed in such a way that Prine knew that's exactly what happened. Lucy's mom made the best pie in the whole state. And Lucy was quite willing to use it as bribery.

"What kind of pie are you going to get?" he asked Bob Carlyle.

"Aw, Tom."

"C'mon, now. You ragged me a little about her. Just the way she bribed you to. So I just want to know what kind of pie you get."

"Well, I guess it don't make any difference if I tell you. Apple."

"With ice cream," Daly said. "Two scoops."

"Same for you, I imagine, Sheriff."

"Blueberry for me. And I ain't ashamed of bein' bribed, because I believe in what I'm sayin'. She'd make you a damned good wife. A much better one than Cassie Neville ever would. And I'm speakin' for Bob when I say that, right, Bob?"

"Right, Sheriff. I wouldn't agree to do it if I didn't believe in what I was sayin'."

"Not even for two pieces of apple pie?"

"Don't forget the ice cream," Daly said.

"Not even for two pieces of apple pie with ice cream, Bob?" Prine said.

"Hell, Tom," Daly said, "if you was nicer to her, you'd get free pie, too."

Prine couldn't take any more matchmaking. He left.

Lucy Killane was having one of her bad days, days that were even more damaging to body and soul than her monthly visitor.

She had walked past the sheriff's office five times today, in hopes of glimpsing Tom Prine. Five times. Today the pain was as fresh as if they'd just broken up last night. Panic — fury — self-pity — confusion — panic again. This was the course of her day. She waited on people at the café, she sat out back and ate lunch with three other café workers, she even went to the hospital just now to get her instructions. But it was as if somebody else had done all these things.

Now she was walking past the sheriff's office for the sixth time and —

— there he was. Coming out of the door. A letter — her letter, she was sure — in his hand.

He saw her and nodded hello.

Her instinct was to run away, flee. It

would be humiliating to see him after writing him such a mushy and forlorn letter, a letter that basically begged him to ask her to stay in town. Not leave.

He didn't wait for her to walk up to him. He walked up to her.

"Haven't had time to read it," he said, holding the letter up.

She could be pretty damned bold sometimes. And right now was a good example. She tore the letter from his fingers.

"Hey," he said, "that's mine."

"No, it isn't," she said. "It's just a silly, stupid letter that belongs to the silly, stupid girl who wrote it."

She froze in place. All street sounds faded — clatter of wagons; shouts of day's end children; corner conversations of loafers and idlers and riffraff; neigh of horse, cry of infant, laughter of flirty young girls. All of it faded and there she stood on some plane of her own making — some plane that displayed her to all as the fool she was.

Prine must have sensed this, because he took her arm and said, "Where you headed?"

"Madame Missy's," she managed to say.

"I'll walk with you."

She didn't object. Couldn't. Needed his

strength now. Had none of her own.

Oh my God Tom why did you quit loving me?

Walking. Him saying, "You're doing the whole town a favor. Checking those prostitutes the way you do."

One of the jobs she had as a hospital volunteer was to visit the two cribs each week and see if any of the girls had rashes, discharges, pain, runny noses and eyes that were bothering them. Syphilis flourished in many — too many — western towns. Her girls liked Lucy and her high spirits and her sympathetic eyes even if the madams didn't. The madams found her an imposition. The only reason they allowed her in was that Sheriff Daly demanded weekly talks with somebody from the hospital. At first doctors and nurses came. But there was something so cold and official and disapproving about them that neither the madams nor the girls would cooperate with them.

Lucy was a compromise. She didn't examine the girls physically, and that helped. And she certainly didn't make moral judgments about the girls. She liked many of them and felt sorry for all of them.

She was gradually beginning to breathe normally, becoming aware again of her surroundings, feeling less embarrassed about having been so open with Tom.

"I think I'll try Denver."

"Denver's a good place for a young woman, Lucy. No doubt about that."

"Or maybe Cheyenne."

"That'd be good, too."

"One of the girls at the café thinks I should try California."

"Hear lots of interesting things about California."

"Then there's always the East."

"There sure is, Lucy. I'd like to see New York myself someday. Stand down on the street and look up at all those tall buildings."

"Another girl said I could get a lot of New York things in Chicago and I wouldn't have to travel as far."

"That's true. And they're planning to have the world's fair there in a few years."

"The world's fair," Lucy said, "imagine that." Then: "Of course, you don't have to even leave the town limits here to see mansions and things. The Nevilles' place —"

"Well, technically that isn't in the town limits, but I see your point." He pressed her arm gently, and they stopped walking for a moment. "So you heard."

"Heard?" All innocence.

"That Cassie Neville invited me out to her place last night."

"Oh, yes — I guess I do sort of remember hearing about that. But it skipped my mind."

"Uh-huh." He smiled and then did the thing she least wanted him to do and the thing she most wanted him to do. Kissed her. Only briefly. Only briefly. But kissed her nonetheless.

"I take it that's what your letter was all about. Me going to the Neville place."

"I guess I did mention it in passing."

"Given that temper of yours," he laughed, "I'll bet it was more than 'in passing.'"

"You know, when I finally get out of here, wherever I go — Chicago or New York or Denver or California — I won't give things like the Nevilles a second thought. I'll be a different person."

She thought — hoped — that he would kiss her again. But he didn't. He just started walking again, taking her along with him.

She said, "You think you'll see her again?"

"Oh, Lucy, please don't ask me things like that."

"I guess you plan to, then."

"We'll just have to see what happens."

Madame Missy's was melancholy in the purple shadows of the growing autumn dusk. A player piano sounded ridiculously merry given Lucy's mood. And Madame Missy herself, who knew everything about everybody who was anybody in Claybank, peeked her Pekingese face between the parted curtains in the front window and took a gander at them.

Lucy knew she'd come undone if she stayed here. She slid her arm from Tom's and said, "Well, I appreciate you walking with me."

"Lucy, I — This is hard for both of us, but —" He stopped himself.

"But what?"

"It's just a selfish thought I have."

"What sort of selfish thought, Tom?"

"I — I just don't want you to leave town. But I can't make any promises if you stay."

So finally it wasn't Lucy who broke away but Tom himself. He said, "You're a fine woman, Lucy. In all respects. Never forget that."

And then he was gone.

CHAPTER EIGHT

Prine didn't sleep well. His dreams alternated between Cassie and Lucy. A man could get confused.

Around three, he became fully awake and there was hell to pay. The nocturnal orchestra of the hotel where he boarded was performing a full symphony. You had your snoring, you had your hawking, you had your rolling, you had your tossing, you had your headboard creaking, you had your amorous sex dream moans, you had your muffled-scream nightmares, you had coughing, scratching, muttering, snorting, and gasping.

What you had, in other words, was just about every kind of prohibition against getting back to sleep you could think of.

Up and down the hall the symphony played, fading, then full again, unceasing.

He sat up and smoked. He lay back down and scratched. He thought. He tried not to think. And then he repeated the entire sequence all over again.

Dawn came haughty and gray, taunting

him with the fact that he wasn't ready for this day. Flesh and bone and blood and sinew were not strong and eager. His mind was dulled, unable to focus sharply.

He didn't need to see Lucy at the café. There was another one a block away. The food wasn't as good, but coffee was what he really wanted anyway.

He'd seen a cartoon once of a man pulling his lower eyelid out and pouring a cup of coffee directly into the eye pouch. He remembered this as he sat in the café, bringing the first cup of coffee to his lips. On the table in front of him were four cigarettes. Last night, unable to sleep, nothing else to do, he went ahead and rolled himself twenty cigarettes.

A number of people nodded to him, but nobody tried to sit down. He kept his expression grim as possible so nobody would be tempted. Carrying on a conversation would be too much of a strain at the moment.

The day came alive despite his best efforts to keep it away. The people in the café headed for work; wagons rumbled on the street outside; a factory whistle blew; the Catholic church rang its bell.

He got up, paid his bill, and forced himself to go to work.

★ ★ ★

"Boy, you look like shit, Tom."

"Thanks, Bob."

"I just mean you look plum wore out. Another romantic night?"

"Afraid not. Just couldn't sleep."

He spent the first fifteen minutes in the office going through the arrest sheets of the night deputy.

"Not much there," Bob Carlyle said. "Lucky he was able to stay awake, a night as slow as that."

One saloon fight. A lost dog (found). A wife-beating (husband arrested). Two public-drunkenness arrests.

"See what you mean, Bob."

Prine hadn't quite finished saying that when the door exploded inward and Mike Perry, the Neville ranch foreman, stood there with a Winchester in one hand and a Colt in the other. He was out of breath.

"Where's the sheriff?"

"Courthouse," Prine said. "He's testifying." He sensed what had happened. He had to be careful to act surprised.

"Miss Neville's been kidnapped," Perry said.

Carlyle was up and out of his chair. "What the hell you talking about?"

"On the way into town this morning.

Her usual trip. She asked me to ride into town with her. She thought a wheel might be loose. I told her it looked fine, but she was nervous about it. So I was right there when he rode up. A man in a mask. Kerchief all the way up to his eyes. Had a sawed-off shotgun. Knocked me out — and I've got one hell of a headache to prove it. Anyway, we need a posse and fast. We can't wait for the sheriff."

"But where the hell would we even start?" Carlyle said. "We need to get organized before we do anything."

"You want me to tell Richard Neville you wouldn't get a posse up till you got 'organized'?"

"We'll be ready in fifteen minutes," Prine said. "But we need you to tell us where it happened and give us the best description you can of the man who took her. What he looked like, sounded like, what kind of horse he was riding." He glanced at Carlyle. "You want to get all this from Mike here, or do you want to round up the posse?"

"You're better with people than I am," Carlyle said. "Why don't you round up the posse?"

And so he did.

He got seven men — the blacksmith, the

freight manager of an overland shipping company, an unemployed sixteen-year-old who had been winning marksmanship contests since he was twelve, a retired deputy eager for action, a railroad man on a weeklong vacation, an auxiliary deputy, and a saloon bouncer.

They joined Carlyle and Mike Perry and swung east to the stage road on which Cassie Neville had been kidnapped.

One of the kidnapper's horses had a shoe that hadn't been fitted quite right. The blacksmith explained what was wrong with it, but nobody paid much attention. The posse wanted to get going. You don't join a posse to get a ten-minute lecture on how to fit a horseshoe properly. You join a posse because you've got a personal stake in it or because it gives you blessed relief from the workaday world or because you think there's at least the possibility that you'll be able to wound or possibly kill somebody legally.

Carlyle was better at geography than Prine, so he assigned the ground he wanted his two-man teams to cover. Prine drew the timberland to the west, where the pine-covered foothills slanted toward the largest river in this part of the state. There was always the possibility, Carlyle said, that they'd taken her to the river where a boat waited. If that was the case, they could be a long ways from here.

They were just about ready to ride off to their appointed search areas when a rider, coming fast, started shouting for them to wait. He was coming from the direction of the Neville ranch. As he drew closer, Prine saw that it was Richard Neville.

The first surprise was that Neville didn't look like Neville. Prine had always seen him in business suits and fancy dress suits, like what he had worn last night. In a faded blue workshirt, Levi's, and a black western hat, he looked like just another cowpuncher. He had a Winchester in his rifle scabbard and a lasso around his saddle horn.

"I missed the first group that went out," Neville said. "I'll go with this bunch if that's all right." He hadn't seemed to notice Prine till now. "Tom Prine. Why don't I go with him?"

"You do whatever you want, Mr. Neville," Carlyle said. "She's your sister."

"All right with you, Prine?" Neville said.

"Fine."

Prine noted that among workingmen

Neville was less showy, even humble. He didn't tell Carlyle what he was going to do. He first asked if it would be all right. Apparently, he was one of those men who knew how to play to each crowd he was with. He needed these men. And they'd quickly resent him if he played the peacock land baron as he had last night.

They set off for the foothills to the west.

The day warmed up. By midmorning, the temperature was in the high sixties. The haze burned off the pines early, too.

They stayed on the road for a long time, watching for the ill-fitted horseshoe pattern the blacksmith had told them about at such length. They saw nothing.

"They either didn't come this way or they stayed off the stage road here," Prine said.

He had to be careful. Because he knew who'd taken her and where she was being held, he had to be very careful. He didn't want to say anything that would make him sound as if he had some knowledge he was keeping from Neville.

Neville had two moods for the first ninety minutes. He was either silent or so angry he could barely shape words.

"When we find them," he said, "I'm going to kill them."

"Well, if it's in self-defense, that'd be fine, Neville. But if it's not — it'd be murder."

"Why should I worry about murder? They sure as hell didn't worry about kidnapping. She's an innocent young girl. I've kept her sheltered all her life. I didn't see any reason for her to get filthy by rubbing up against the rest of the world."

"She must've picked up a few things working in the church basement."

Neville frowned. "Do-gooder stuff. She doesn't have to live with them. Get to know them. She gets to hand out food and clothing and feel that she's doing something with her life. Then she runs right back to our house with the servants and all the luxuries."

Neville probably didn't even know how contemptuous he sounded. She was his little sister, a pretty piece of fluff he needed to protect because that was what honorable gentlemen did — protected pretty pieces of fluff. Prine was resentful. Cassie was such a part of his imagination now that he wanted to defend her. Say that she was a grown woman and a smart one and a good one. Say that she had a laugh like music and eyes that you couldn't ever forget. Not ever.

But he knew better, of course. He rode on.

Just after noon, they reached the timberland. Prine himself had a few bad moments — doubt and fear that maybe he'd done the wrong thing. Maybe he should have stopped this kidnapping the moment he found out about it. What if she tried to escape and got killed in the process? It was possible. Things went wrong all the time. All the time.

Neville's shout jerked Prine from his thoughts.

Neville drew his horse up short and flung himself from his saddle. He was a lot rougher man than Prine would have guessed from meeting him at the recital. He looked comfortable with a six-gun and even more comfortable with his fists.

By the time Prine dismounted, Neville had hunched down over something in a patch of crusty soil and said, "Shit."

Then he was up on his feet, scowling.

"Thought I saw that damned crooked horseshoe print."

"You need to relax. That's the best thing you can do for yourself right now."

Neville scowled. You could see the calculation in his eyes. He wasn't sure he could whip Prine, but he was about ready to try. Then he took a deep breath and visibly relaxed. "I don't always treat her the way I should, Prine. And she resents it. And I promise not to do it anymore. And then I go right on treating her like this little child. But for all of that, I love her. I love her more than anything on this earth." Anger seized him again. "So it's not real easy to relax. Not when you love somebody the way I love her."

He stalked back to his horse and rode off.

Prine gave him some time alone and then caught up with him.

Neville surprised him by saying, "Sorry I ran my mouth back there. I guess I forgot you want to find her as much as I do."

"I sure do," Prine said. "I sure do."

By the time he got done testifying in court, Sheriff Daly had missed not only both posses but also the chance to talk to Richard Neville.

One of Neville's men came to the sheriff's office a few minutes after he returned from the courthouse.

Hank Cummings was the man's name. He probably changed clothes sometimes, but Daly could never remember seeing him in anything other than the faded blue workshirt, the faded blue Levi's, and the faded white hat that was now the color of sweat and dirt.

"They swung out by the ranch to see where she was kidnapped. Guy hit Mike Perry pretty hard."

"Mike Perry? He doesn't usually ride with her into town, does he?"

"Not usually. But she was worried about a loose wheel."

"Bob Carlyle left me a note. I've lost three hours. No use trying to catch them now." With the sole of his Texas boot, he shoved a chair in Cummings's direction. "Sit down a spell."

"Sure."

"I want to know a few things about the ranch. That's why I wish I could talk to Neville."

"Well, I'll help you any way I can."

Daly resorted to his briar; Cummings started rolling a cigarette.

"Neville fire anybody lately?" Daly said.

"Not that I've heard of."

"Anybody been giving him trouble? Some old enemy?"

"Nope. Mike Perry bunks with all the boys, and he always tells us what's going on with 'the mister,' as the boys call him. He hasn't said anything about any enemies."

"Any cowhand seem to have it in for him?"

Cummings grinned, his ancient, weathered face showing the boy that lingered somewhere inside him. "You asking me to speak out of school, Sheriff?"

"Out of school?"

"You asking me what the boys — and I'm including Mike Perry here — really think of Neville?"

Daly drew on his lighted pipe, savored the taste of tobacco. "They don't like him, huh?"

"You ever met many people who do?"

Daly smiled. "I see what you mean."

"If you're askin' if he's well-liked, hell no, he isn't. But if you're askin' if one of the boys would kidnap Miss Cassie, hell no, they wouldn't. You got to remember, most of the boys on the Bar Double N have been there ten, twenty years. A couple of them's been there almost thirty. They helped raise Miss Cassie. She's the opposite of her brother. She calls most of 'em 'uncle.' Uncle Bob and Uncle Bill and so on. Most of the hands never had time to get married or raise a family, so they sort of adopted her. They might do a number of things if they got pissed off enough at Neville — but they'd never touch Miss Cassie. Never."

115

Daly had his feet up on the desk. "Well, it doesn't have to be anybody from the ranch. I always try to look at the people around them first. But there've been so damned many kidnappings lately. A couple of convicts get out of prison with no money and no prospects, they start reading the papers to see who's got some money. And then right away they go after their child."

"That's probably what happened here."

Daly nodded. "Probably." Then: "How about Cassie? She have any enemies?"

Cummings snorted. "Cassie? Who'd have anything against Cassie? For one thing, even though she's lived here all her life, she's never really met a lot of people. The mister kept her pretty much sheltered since their father died. I expect this is just the kind of thing he was afraid of."

"Kidnapping?"

"Or rape. That's where an old enemy might fit in. Kidnap the mister's sister and rape her. The mister would go crazy. You don't see many suitors around Cassie, and that's why. He wants her to stay pure as long as he can. Right up to her wedding day. He knows he'll have to marry her off eventually. But until then, she's pretty much under his thumb."

"Then if it isn't a ranch hand and it isn't an angry suitor — we're probably back to some drifters who thought they saw an easy way to make some money."

"I don't like that choice at all."

"Neither do I," Daly said. "Those're the kind of men who end up killing the girls they steal."

CHAPTER NINE

The ride back at day's end was long and mostly silent, both men, Prine and Neville, given to their own thoughts and feelings. They'd gone all the way to the major river in the area and found nothing.

Now, hungry shadows gathering for the feast of night, they came to the outskirts of Claybank.

Neville said, "Maybe they found her. Maybe she's all right." The hope in his voice sounded young, naive. Prine was surprised he was capable of that kind of desperate hope. Neville seemed too hard and manipulative for that sort of self-delusion. But then, it was his sister and it was clear that he loved her despite the way he treated her. Or maybe he thought that the way he treated her proved that he loved her. Proved it at least to himself.

Both men were tired, dusty, in need of hot food, a place to park their asses that wasn't as unforgiving as a saddle, and time to share thoughts and theories with other members of the posses dispatched today.

118

At suppertime, Claybank moved slow. The stores were closed. Only the occasional wagon clattered its way through town. Even the saloons seemed tame by normal standards.

They headed straight for the sheriff's office. Sheriff Daly's big dun was at the hitching post. He was still saddled, meaning Daly had just gotten back or was ready to go home.

Daly and Bob Carlyle were pouring bourbon into their cups of coffee when Prine and Neville came in. The calm way they greeted the men meant that nobody had found Cassie — dead or alive.

"You two have any luck?" Daly said.

Prine shook his head. "They didn't head for the river. Not that we could see, anyway."

"I'm posting a ten-thousand-dollar reward right now," Neville said. "I should've done it before we left town."

Daly looked him over. "I didn't recognize you when you came in here, you know. Never saw you turned out like this."

Neville's voice was bitter. "You think because I have a lot of money, I just sit home counting it? I work hard, Sheriff."

"I didn't mean anything by that, Richard."

Neville shrugged. "I suppose you didn't. But I get tired of people implying that I'm some kind of pantywaist. I'm good with a rope and a gun. And I can hog-tie a steer fast enough to get me into a rodeo."

Daly handed him the pint bottle of bourbon. "Why don't you suck on the witch's tit and see if you can calm yourself down, Richard?"

Prine was surprised to see Neville guzzle the liquor. No mincing little sip. Probably swallowed one-eighth of the bottle in a single gulp. Neville handed the bottle back to the sheriff, then wiped his mouth with the back of his hand.

Daly held the bottle up in Prine's direction. Prine shook his head.

"You'll probably have a letter waiting for you at your house," Daly said to Neville. "They'll tell you how much and they'll say where they want it delivered. If you want my advice, you'll pay them."

"Of course I'll pay them." Neville looked angry. "You think I wouldn't pay for my own sister?"

"Some people won't."

"Well, they don't have Cassie for a sister. I'd pay any amount they want."

"Don't be surprised if it's a lot of money."

"I just want her back." Neville nodded to Prine. "Then I'm going to ask you for the loan of your deputy here and we're going to hunt them down."

"I'm not sure I can do that," Daly said.

"You want to see them brought to justice, don't you?"

"Of course I do, Richard. But Prine here's a town employee. I can't hire him out freelance."

"What if I was to give the town a gift? I'll bet the mayor would let him go with me if I gave the town a generous gift."

"No offense, Richard. But Prine here's no manhunter. He's a town deputy. You'd be better off getting yourself a tracker or a bounty hunter. Those boys are used to work like that."

Prine, seeing that their disagreement might soon turn into an argument, both men being of the stubborn variety, said, "Why don't we worry about that when the time comes. Right now, Neville should go home and see if there's a ransom letter waiting. It's too late to do anything about it tonight. But why don't we all meet back here at eight this morning and make our plans then?"

Neville clapped Prine on the back. "Good idea. I need some rest, anyway." He glanced at all three of them. "I'll see you men tomorrow."

Prine settled in to look through his mail. Nothing interesting. He poured himself a cup of Davis's molten coffee and asked what the various teams of men had discovered.

"Not a hell of a lot," Daly said.

Prine carefully asked about several places they might have looked, working in the Knowles's farmhouse as casually as possible.

Carlyle joined in at that point. "There're four deserted farmhouses in the area. Men went through every one of them and didn't find anything."

"There's a root cellar at the Knowles place," Prine said. "They look there, too?"

"Looked everywhere. No sign of her."

Prine went back to his paperwork eventually. Or appeared to, anyway. Couldn't concentrate, of course. His stomach was tense and filled with acid. His throat with bile. He'd figured all along that they'd hide her in one of the many caves around the Knowles farmhouse. Way too many of those to check out. Then, at nightfall, they'd move her into the farmhouse and the root cellar.

But what if they hadn't? What if they'd changed their minds, figured that there was a better place to hide her? Then what?

There would go his reward. There would go his prominence. There would go his dream.

He made a show of being hungry. Three, four times over the course of the next hour, he talked about food. Finally, Daly said, "You convinced me, Tom. I'm headin' home to supper."

"Me, too," Carlyle said.

"Ryan's making his early rounds," Daly said. "You can lock up and leave if you want to."

"Might as well wait for him," Prine said.

"Thought you were so damned hungry," Daly said.

"I am, but I don't want to face this paperwork in the morning."

Daly shrugged. "Up to you."

They left.

All Prine accomplished while he waited for Harry Ryan, the night deputy, was working himself into a higher state of alarm. There was probably nothing to worry about. Probably everything was fine. Probably just about now they'd be moving her into the root cellar. Probably they would have delivered the ransom note and were now just waiting till morning to pick up the money. Probably.

But Prine couldn't let go of all the ways his plan could fail. Hell, it didn't take much imagination to think that they'd found a new and better place to hide her. He could remember his surprise that they picked a place so open and obvious. He could hear them making the argument for open and obvious — the posse would look at it early in their search, find it empty, move on, and then never bother them again. But it was still a perilous place to be should someone decide to recheck it the next day.

Prine wished he hadn't agreed to wait for Harry Ryan. Where the hell was he, anyway?

Prine got up and started pacing. That was a bad sign. Pacing was something he did only when everything started to overwhelm him. . . .

Half an hour later, Harry Ryan came striding in. A large, square, affable man with a drinker's nose that was almost as scarlet as his hair, he said, "Hey, Tom, you didn't have to wait for me."

"That's all right. I had a lot of paperwork to do."

"Hell, you coulda just locked up and left. I woulda."

"Wasn't any trouble." Prine was back at

124

his desk, pretending to be absorbed with all his paperwork. He stood up and yawned.

Ryan didn't have a desk of his own. There wasn't much inside work on the night shift. Mostly you ran in unruly drunks. He always sat at Daly's desk. "Say, I ran into Timmins over to the hardware store and he told me to tell Daly something. Maybe you could pass it along in the morning and save me the trouble of writin' it down."

Prine had seen some of Ryan's notes. He was barely literate and his notes not very understandable.

"Sure, what is it?" Prine said, heading for the door.

"Said a couple mornings when he was sweeping off the sidewalk, he seen this man watching Cassie Neville come into town on her buggy. Said the man used a stopwatch, like he wanted to know exactly what time she got here every morning. Sounds like one of the kidnappers to me."

"Could be," Prine said, trying to keep his voice neutral. He didn't know if this would help or hurt his plan. Probably it wouldn't have any effect on it one way or the other. Still, it gave him an anxious feeling. "He describe the man?"

"He sure did."

And boy did he. A description that detailed was just about as good as a photograph.

"You be sure and tell him, Tom."

"Don't worry," Prine said. "I will."

He walked over to his horse, mounted up, and headed for the farmhouse and the root cellar.

The evening rush had started early at The Friendly Café. Lucy was asked to stay for a few extra hours to help out. Maybe it was tonight's cold weather, a large number of only occasional customers coming in for the kind of food they couldn't get at home.

Lucy was leaving work just as Harry Ryan cut across the street a block away to enter the sheriff's office. She recognized his silhouette by his size and by his long stride. Not many men could eat up ground the way Harry could.

She convinced herself to walk past the sheriff's office so she could say hello to Harry. Tom would be gone by now, in his room probably, or maybe out for a few beers.

He wouldn't be out with Cassie Neville.

She felt ashamed of not fearing for Cassie. It wasn't Cassie's fault that Tom no longer loved Lucy. It wasn't Cassie's fault that Lucy couldn't deal well with her loss of Tom. It wasn't Cassie's fault that she was rich and beautiful.

Lucy said a quick and sincere prayer for Cassie. That she'd be found soon. Alive and well.

When she reached Harry, she said, "Any word on Cassie Neville, Harry?"

"Oh, evening, Lucy. Afraid not. Nothing new, anyway."

"I just said a prayer for her."

"Everybody's praying. All the churches had special services for her this afternoon."

Harry touched his hat and went inside. In the open door, she saw Tom bent over his desk, working, and that combination of thrill and terror went through her with icy panic.

She didn't know which was worse. That he might see her in the dusk out here. Or that he might not see her.

She hesitated a moment, fighting the urge to go up to the door and slip inside, pretending that she didn't know Tom was in there. But no. No, she wouldn't do it. She had to get control of herself. This was a form of madness, and she knew it. There were articles in some of the women's magazines about how spurned women sometimes gave in to melancholia that led to insanity or suicide or murder. She didn't feel that she was close to any of these things yet. But it wasn't impossible to imagine that she might get there someday.

She hurried on to the livery stable. She needed to get a horse tonight. After supper, she planned to go to visit a patient whom she'd befriended at the hospital, an old miner who was dying of a bad heart.

The stable stank of old hay, road apples, horse, and the rain-soaked wood that had comprised the livery since shortly after the town had been built. She had stopped by here this morning, so the liveryman had a roan all picked out for her. He got it saddled and turned it over. She was good with horses. They generally seemed to like her as much as she liked them.

When she came out onto the street, she saw Tom mounting his own horse in front of the sheriff's office. Again, her compulsion was to make him aware of her somehow. Catch up to him as if she didn't know it was him. Or fall in beside him and simply wish him good evening. Just a casual encounter.

But she knew it would be more than that. It always was. And it was always her fault for letting it become more than that.

She just sat her horse, watching Tom

move his animal away from the office. She wondered where he was going. East. Why would he be headed east? She tried to think of whom he might know in that direction.

She sat there for some time, thinking. And then she slowly began moving away from the livery, taking, at a good distance, the same route Tom was taking.

She was barely aware of what she was doing. She was almost trancelike. Her eyes saw but didn't see. Her ears heard but didn't hear. Her breath came in sharp little gasps. Where was she going? What was she doing? My Lord, he would hate her if he ever found out that she'd started following him like this.

He would hate her for sure.

Prine didn't become aware of the rider behind him until he reached the top of the hill that looked down on the farmhouse where Cassie was being kept. Or where he hoped she was being kept, anyway.

No light in the house, of course. Moonlight silvered the windows. An awning swung in the wind, banging against the window frame. A wild dog sniffed around the autumn-scorched grass in the front yard.

He heard the horse before seeing it. A narrow, rock-bottomed creek ran in the distance behind him. Horseshoes clicked against stone, announcing the arrival of horse and rider.

Prine yanked his Winchester from his scabbard, spurred his animal in among the shallow stand of jackpines to hide.

The rider was in no hurry to crest the hill. The horse was loping at best. All sorts of names and faces flashed through Prine's mind. Would the sheriff have followed him? Bob Carlyle? Maybe Richard Neville himself? Had somebody followed him previously and figured out what he was up to?

The scent of pine sap strong in his nostrils, Prine watched as a lone rider appeared in a bald patch on the top of the hill, just about where he'd sat his own horse. He sniffled. Pine sap always played hell with his sinuses.

His eyes refused at first to believe what his mind told him was true. A woman sat the horse.

She dropped down from her mount, ground-tying her animal and walking closer to the rim of the hill so she could see below.

Why would a woman follow him out here?

He was about to find out, because he sneezed just then. The damned pinecone. Giving away his position.

The woman, bold, turned back toward him and said, "Who's there?" Speaking to the darkened stand of jackpines in front of her.

He recognized her now. "Lucy? Lucy, what the hell are you doing out here?"

"Is that you, Tom?"

He nudged his horse out from the jackpines, dropped down out of the saddle.

As he approached her, she said, "Oh, gosh, Tom. I'm such a fool. I — I swear it was almost like I couldn't help myself. I saw you leaving town. I was leaving, too. And I just started to follow you."

"Then you turn right around and go back to town. I'm working tonight, and you shouldn't be here."

Lucy said, "You think she could be down there? Wouldn't they have checked it earlier today?"

He was angry she looked so lovely in the moonlight. Maybe if she hadn't looked so good — evoking both his appreciative eye for female beauty and his guilt for leaving her — maybe then he would've been able to put her on her horse and send her back. But he couldn't.

131

Plus there was the matter of what she'd been able to surmise. He had to keep her quiet about this.

He said, "I have to trust you with something."

"You know you can trust me, Tom."

"I swung past here this afternoon and I thought I saw three horses in the woods in back of the place. They may be keeping her in there. I wanted to wait till nightfall to find out."

"Why didn't you bring some help?"

"I don't want a shoot-out. They might kill Cassie if it came to that."

"I guess that's true."

He took her by the waist and drew her to him as he had so many other times. She was woman-warm in the chill night, her flesh feeling right and good beneath her jacket. "This is something that's between us, all right, Lucy? You didn't see me tonight. I'll just tell the sheriff that I was riding out to see Bob Carlyle's house when I saw a light in the place and decided to swing by."

"Sure, Tom."

And then, without any warning, she kissed him. Sliding her arms around his neck. Pulling him toward her with hard, childlike need. And he responded, remembering how good and tender a love she was. How playful she was at times. Again, like a child. And how many nights lying beside her he'd get caught up in her out-loud daydreams of the day when they had two or three children and Tom had gone into some safe business and was making a good name for himself. How easy it had been to share her sense of their destiny then. But always at the back of his mind there'd been a greater dream. And now, with any luck at all, that dream was about to be realized. A hero, a reward, a beautiful, rich girl.

He eased her away from him.

"So I've got to depend on you, Lucy."

"You know you can," she said, still shaken from their kiss.

"Get on your horse and head right back to town."

She nodded. And then kissed him as impulsively as she had the first time.

He watched her for a good half-mile, till he was sure she wouldn't double back and surprise him again.

Then he tied his horse to a jackpine branch, grabbed his Winchester, and proceeded to the west, so that he could come up behind the farmhouse when he approached it.

CHAPTER TEN

Prine found road apples but no horses in the timber behind the farmhouse. He poked the apples with a stick. Fresh — not over three, four hours old. No posse would have put up in the timber here. That meant Tolan and Rooney had been here. But where were they now? And was Cassie all right? Had something happened and they had to flee?

Again, he thought of all the ways kidnappings went wrong sometimes.

He crouched and began his run across the grassy expanse between timber and farmhouse.

Despite the cool night, he was sweating hard by the time he reached the door. Nerves, mostly, and he knew it.

No trouble getting in. In fact, the damned back door nearly fell off its rusted hinges when he opened up. It also squawked like a parrot. It was a good thing he didn't give a damn about making noise.

The stench of the interior gagged him for a moment. Every kind of animal, large and small, that God had ever created had used this deserted place as a toilet. And some of them had died in here, of disease or nocturnal battles. Rain had stenched the wood, too; it smelled — there was no other way to say it — of the grave.

The house: kitchen, dining room, living area. Gutted by time, animals, and most likely hoboes since it wasn't too far from the tracks. For the 'boes this would be like dying and going straight to heaven. A roof over your head every night, even if it was leaky, was hard to beat.

The varieties of feces beneath his boots were hard as bullets. He crunched and crushed and cracked them as he went about searching for the trapdoor that would take him to the root cellar.

He moved through moonlit shadow, kicking aside newspapers, animal shit, odds and ends of the clothing as he searched for the outline of the trapdoor. Once, he thought he heard something below him, but he couldn't be sure.

He returned to the kitchen. That seemed the most logical place for the trapdoor. The farm wife doing a lot of her canning work up here and then carrying it down the ladder to the root cellar.

He got down on all fours and began moving his gloved hands quickly over every inch of kitchen floor. But nothing.

He did the same thing in the dining room and the living room. But again, nothing.

He was just about to walk back to the kitchen when he saw the closet off the dining room. He hadn't looked in there. But when he thought about it, he remembered that some of the early settlers constructed root cellar-like places where they could hole up during Indian attacks. Such places were dangerous. They made the white folk prisoners in a very real way. And if the Indians decided to set fire to the house, the people in the cellar could die from smoke. But when you were outnumbered, as was so often the case — just as the blue uniforms would soon enough outnumber the Indians — a cellar like that was better than standing in the middle of your living room.

In the closet, he found the trapdoor.

Lantern light flickered around the edges where it didn't close flush. Somebody must be down there.

He shoved the barrel of his Winchester down the opening and said, "This is Tom Prine and I'm a deputy sheriff. If anybody's down there, come to the ladder with your hands up. And right now."

"Oh, Tom!"

The voice was unmistakable. And, moments later, the woman was standing at the bottom of the ladder, looking up at him.

"C'mon up, Cassie," Prine said. "I'm taking you home."

"But Tom —"

"C'mon up, Cassie. I want to get you outside before they come back."

She wore a white blouse and brown butternuts that were covered with dirt. Her blond hair was mussed, but not so mussed that, even under these conditions, she'd lost her beauty. Her face, dirt-streaked, was still radiant.

He wasted no time when she emerged from the cellar, her lantern in hand. Beneath her the opening was dark.

He took her hand and guided her through the back half of the house to the sweet smell of the night and the bloom of moonlight on the entire landscape.

Only then did he relax enough to ask all the obvious questions.

"Did they hurt you?"

"No."

"Did they — touch you in any way?"

"No."

"Did they threaten to kill you?"

She didn't look right, didn't look as if she'd been under the frightening strain

137

that went along with being held for ransom. She looked . . . uneasy — as if there were something she needed to tell him but couldn't quite form the words.

"Tom, listen," she said, taking his hand, jolting him with the thrill he'd experienced a few other times with her. "I have to tell you something and trust you to keep it secret."

My Lord, what was she going to tell him? He was perplexed and half afraid to hear it.

"This kidnapping, Tom. It was my idea. I set the whole thing up myself."

When he still hadn't spoken a full minute later, she once more took his hand and said, "Aren't you going to say anything, Tom?"

But there was nothing to say. And this time there was no thrill in holding her hand at all.

"I ever tell you how pretty you are?" the old miner said to Lucy.

"I seem to remember you saying somethin' like that a few times, Clem."

"I hate seein' you, because when I do I wanna be young again. And Lord knows that ain't gonna happen."

"You need to hold still, Clem. I need to check your heart."

"How come you ain't got one of them new ones?"

"Hospital can't afford it. They gave me the old-fashioned kind." Clem referred to the part-wood stethoscope she used. "Now, be quiet or I'll have to get tough with you."

He grinned toothlessly. "That'll be the day."

She checked his pulse, his heart rate, his temperature. Then she spent ten minutes trying to clean up the cabin. Clem could live in a latrine — which he came darned close to doing — and it wouldn't bother him. He'd had one glass window, but that was smashed; rain poured through the roof; and the dirt floor hadn't been worked on in years. His food was usually about to turn deadly by the time she threw it out, and his clothes were stiff with dirt. He had an ancient tomcat who was just as unwholesome as he was. The thing was so scabbed up, scarred up, cut up that she assumed it went out and fought mountain lions at night. And probably kicked the hell out of them.

She was just checking to see if the bread she'd brought Clem last time had started to turn green anywhere when he said, "You don't look happy tonight, Lucy. And I'll bet it's that darned boyfriend of yours."

The bread would do for a while yet. Not that it would matter to Clem Randall. She set it down on the small, cluttered, wobbly table where he seemed to pile everything — a simianlike man of no more than five-two and one hundred twenty pounds who moved with an elbow-cocked swagger that reminded her of a twelve-year-old pretending he was a gunfighter.

She came over and said, "He's just confused is all, Clem. Don't call him my 'darned' boyfriend, all right?"

His dark eyes gleamed. In the lamplight they looked like glass. "You're loyal after he broke your heart. You're a true-blue gal, Lucy. I'll say that for you."

She went over and sat next to him in the rocking chair by the kerosene stove. The fumes had darkened the walls years before. "I think he may be in trouble, Clem."

"Eh? What kind of trouble?"

"I'd better not say. He tried to explain it to me, but he was nervous. His voice had a tremble in it. He sounded sort of scared. I'm afraid for him, Clem, I really am. He's got these dreams —"

"What sort of dreams, youngster?"

"Oh, you know, the usual thing. Money

and being somebody important and all that."

He had a crone's laugh, old Clem, almost a cackle. "Well, now, I'll tell you somethin', Lucy. If men didn't have dreams like that they'd never accomplish anything. They'd sit around on their lazy backsides and let somebody else do all the work. You think I woulda mined all them years if I didn't have a dream like that? I can't fault him for that, Lucy. And you shouldn't, either."

"I don't. It's just . . ."

"Just what?"

"Well, when you're a lawman you have certain temptations . . ."

He stared at her, not speaking for a time. "Maybe usin' his badge in a way he shouldn't ought to, you mean."

"Yes."

"I can see where it'd be temptin', have to say that. A lawman has a better chance of gettin' away with a crime than somebody like me does, that's for sure."

She checked her watch. She needed to be getting on home. She stood up. "Thanks for listening to me, Clem. And I'd appreciate it if you didn't tell anybody anything I said."

That high-pitched crone's laugh again.

"You don't have to worry about me, youngster. Nobody ever comes out to see me anyway, 'ceptin' you and this old Pawnee fella I've known since I came out here. And all he wants to talk about is who's gonna get my cabin when I die. I guess he thinks since he spent so much time puttin' up with me, it's his by squatter's rights."

She kissed him on the forehead. The sticky forehead. Someday she planned to drop him into a tub of water and work on him head to toe with soap and a scrub brush until she raised welts.

"G'night, Clem."

"G'night, Lucy. You say a prayer for me and I'll say a prayer for you. How's that?"

She smiled. "I couldn't ask for better than that."

"I'm getting cold," Cassie said.

Prine had moved away from her, perched himself on a small boulder near the timber. He rolled himself a cigarette.

"Aren't you going to say anything, Tom?"

"What am I supposed to say?"

"That you understand. That you don't think I'm just a foolish little rich girl. That you don't hate me. The only reason I did this was so that my brother would notice me. Maybe value me a little. I didn't do this for selfish reasons."

He got his cigarette going and thought for a moment. There was no sense hurting her feelings. She was doing a good job of that herself. She was trying to justify a stupid, reckless act and having a hard time doing it.

The romance of her was gone. When he looked at her there in the moonlight, she didn't even look so pretty anymore. Just dirt-smeared and sort of pathetic. No allure at all in standing near an outhouse that had been turned on its side and an ancient wagon with only three wheels.

"You wanted Richard's attention," he said. "You got it. And I feel sorry for him. He damned near came undone this afternoon. Judging by what I saw today, I'd say he loves you a lot more than you think he does."

She walked up and down to keep warm. "You're seeing it from the outside. You're not seeing how he orders me around and never takes me seriously and makes up these stupid rules. I'm an adult, and he doesn't seem to understand that. I just wanted to teach him a lesson, scare him a little. Maybe he'll appreciate me now."

He couldn't resist. "Do you have any idea how much turmoil you've caused today? How worried people are? I don't think an adult would do anything like that."

"Oh, fine, now you sound just like Richard. So high and mighty all the time. Why don't you just leave?"

"Not without you."

"Well, for your information, I'm not going anywhere. Tolan and Rooney are coming back. They're my partners in this, remember?"

"How'd you meet those two, anyway?"

"Tolan came to the church basement one afternoon. He was looking for a winter coat. I'd had this idea for some time. I think he has a little crush on me. He kept coming back. One day I told him about the idea. We're friends, sort of."

"Some friends, Cassie. These are dangerous men. Ruthless."

"They haven't hurt me, have they?"

He flipped his cigarette into the darkness, watched as it struck a tree, disintegrated into a dozen stars. "You're coming back with me. Now."

"You're not my boss."

"Looks like somebody needs to be." He sounded, and felt, disgusted. He was tired of her whining, tired of her dramatics. "Let's get going."

The Colt came from the front of her butternuts. Tucked behind her blouse. "Head back to town, Tom. Now. You keep my secret and I'll see that you get the reward. That's more than somebody like you'll see in the next thirty years if you're lucky."

The scorn for workingmen was clear in her "somebody like you" remark. He'd been around rich people enough to know that many of them divided the world into two groups — peers and everybody else. And "everybody else" fell into the category of servants. Even if you weren't in livery, they used you anyway. Sometimes they paid you; other times they forced you to do it free. But one way or the other, you did their bidding. And sometimes you didn't even know about it.

"I need you to drop your Colt and your Winchester, Tom."

"Do you know what the hell you're doing?"

"I know exactly what I'm doing. I don't want you coming back here threatening Tolan and Rooney. They just went to have a few beers. But they'll be here soon. I've got my cash payment ready for them. I don't want anything to go wrong here. So I'm taking your guns. You head back and sit on the outskirts of town. I'll meet you there. I've got a horse in the barn over there. Then we can ride into town together and I'll tell everybody you rescued me."

He hadn't complied with her request for his guns. She reminded him of this by stepping close to him and bringing the barrel of the Colt down hard across his cheek. She was capable of much more force than he realized.

"Your guns, Tom."

He would've fought back, but what was the point? As much as he despised her now, he despised himself even more. Going against all his principles to make it appear that he'd "rescued" her so that he could get the reward and maybe her hand. He was just as foolish, just as selfish, just as mercenary as she was. A good lawman would've broken up the "kidnapping" before it happened.

The sharp wind was beginning to freeze his nose and give him an earache. He just wanted away from here, away from her. If only he could get away from himself, too.

"Don't bother with the reward," he said. "Just ride back to town and tell everybody you got yourself free."

"I'm going to pretend I don't know who kidnapped me. I want you to go along with that, too." An ironic smile. "I'm a lot smarter than you thought, aren't I?"

"Not smarter," he said. "Just more foolish. And I'm even more foolish than you are."

He dropped Winchester and Colt on the ground. "I want my guns back. You know where I live."

"You'll have them tonight."

He climbed up on his horse, weary, addled, sorrowful. Not until now did he realize his true nature. He was a con, a grifter, just like so many of the men he'd arrested over the years.

He swung his horse westward and, without saying anything, headed back to town.

Chapter Eleven

Prine spent a mostly sleepless night. He realized that while he'd always been a law-abiding man, he'd never been a good one.

All it took was the temptation of a reward and he forgot everything he supposedly knew about morality.

Cassie no longer mattered to him. She had her own life. He wouldn't tell anybody anything about the kidnapping — not for her sake but for his. If Sheriff Daly ever found out what he'd done, he'd fire Prine for sure. And let every lawman he knew know just how much a risk Prine was as a lawman.

He didn't delude himself. Part of his shame was his anxiety over being found out. Cassie could always say the wrong thing. Richard could start taking a closer look at the entire incident and begin to expose it. Tolan and Rooney could ask for more money to be silent — and where would something like that end?

Dawn found Prine in a wooden chair, a big gray tomcat in his lap, watching

Claybank begin, groggy and reluctant, to awaken.

He shaved, washed up, dressed, and headed for The Friendly Café. He felt ridiculously happy to see Lucy.

She brought him his first cup of coffee.

"You didn't get much sleep last night, did you?"

"Not much."

She leaned in so she could whisper.

"And you didn't tell me the truth about what was going on out at that farmhouse, did you?"

He stared at his coffee cup.

"Are you in trouble, Tom? D'you need to get out of town? I've got a few dollars put by. . . ."

He touched her hand.

"Did I ever tell you how sweet you are, Lucy?"

"Not for a long time."

"Well, I'm telling you now. And I'm going to tell you every single day from now on."

She did something she'd never done before — knew she shouldn't have done. She sat down at his table. Serving women were never supposed to sit with customers while on duty.

"You're in trouble, Tom. And I'm afraid

for you. But that's not a reason to come back to me. You know I love you. But right now's not a good time to try and make up. You have to be a man and face up to whatever you've done."

He laughed. "You sound like one of the nuns at Catholic school. Be a man and face up to whatever you've done. They told me that the day I broke the school window with a baseball. They couldn't figure out who'd done it. So they held up class until the guilty party confessed."

"Maybe that's what you need to do now, Tom. Confess."

"If you mean confession, it's been a while."

"Not necessarily confession to a priest. But to somebody. You need to talk about the trouble you're in and how you think you can handle it."

"That makes sense, I guess."

"Maybe you could talk to Sheriff Daly."

"Maybe he's the man I need to talk to," Prine said.

Prine hadn't thought of that before, but now that Lucy had brought up the subject, it sounded like a good idea.

Tell Daly what he'd done. Take responsibility for it. Tell Daly he'd like to stay and show him how good a lawman he could be.

But what would Daly say? He wasn't an especially forgiving man, but he wasn't merciless, either. Maybe he'd understand how a young, dreamy lawman could get caught up in living out his dream. . . .

Prine guessed that was probably the best way to handle it. Instead of trying to keep his involvement in the kidnap secret, just tell Daly what had happened. Even if he fired Tom — even if he threatened to bring charges against him — Tom would feel better with the whole situation out in the open.

"I need to get back to work," Lucy said. "But please think about talking to Daly. Maybe he won't be as rough on you as you think."

"That's a good idea, Lucy. And that's just what I'm going to do as soon as I finish my coffee here."

Sheriff Daly and Bob Carlyle were already at their desks. The morning usually began with the three lawmen making out the list of what they needed to do that day. They shared the lists to make sure there wasn't any duplication and that they weren't needed on other jobs.

Prine knew he'd have to wait for Carlyle to leave before he could talk to Daly. He'd made up his mind for sure now. This was the best way. Straightforward and honest. Maybe Daly would be in a forgiving mood once he knew that Cassie was safe. Prine assumed she hadn't gone back home yet. If she had, they'd have known about it by now.

Carlyle stood up, stretched, yawned. "It's funny that you like sleep the older you get, when that's all you're gonna do after you die."

"Maybe this is like a warm-up," Daly said. "Learnin' how to sleep for longer periods of time."

Prine managed to make a joke. "It sure is a lot of fun hanging around with you two. What're you going to talk about next? Somebody getting his innards cut out?"

"The lad thinks we're morbid, Sheriff," Carlyle said.

"Hell, he already knew that. The tales we tell around here . . ."

"Yeah," Carlyle said, "and at least half of them are true." He tapped a piece of paper. "Note here says Riley's hardware was broken into last night. Guess I better get over there and listen to Riley tear me a new one about how law 'n' order's goin' to hell in this town."

"Just remind Riley that when those twins

of his get going, they're responsible for most of the arrests on Saturday night," Daly said. "Damned animals."

Carlyle went over, scooped his hat from its peg, cinched it on, and said, "You'll probably hear Riley shoutin' from two blocks away."

The time was here.

Prine's bowels felt cold and sick. His stomach burned. This wasn't going to be easy. He started to speak, but then the door opened and the woman from the courthouse, Emma Hampton, peeked in and placed a copy of today's court docket on Daly's desk. He'd missed a few appearances over the years. The judges decided it was best to give him a copy of the daily docket. That way it wouldn't ever happen again. And, to date, it hadn't.

After she was gone, Prine stood up and walked over to Carlyle's desk. If he parked himself on its corner, he had a good straight view of Daly.

Daly was writing furiously. He despised paperwork. The scratching of his pen tip had a violent sound to it. Prine knew better than to interrupt him. Daly didn't look up once.

Finally, he set his pen down and said, "This had better be good. Man has a hell of a time concentrating when somebody's hanging off the corner of his eye the way you were."

"It's good, all right," Prine said. "Too good, actually."

For the first time — probably more because of his tone of voice than his words — Daly looked interested. "Somethin's been gnawin' on you these past few days. Probably a good thing to talk it out, lad."

Prine had been all ready to go. To state his case simply. Not to offer any excuses. Not to play for any sympathy. Simple and straightforward.

But when he opened his mouth to speak, he spoke only silence.

"You all right, Tom?"

That was all he had time to say, because just then the door popped open and Wyn Grover, who owned the livery, said, "Stu Byner's just pullin' into town in his wagon, Sheriff. You better come take a look at what he's bringin'."

Grover, a slender man given to drama — he was legendary for tearing into the town council for not much reason at all — wasn't the sort to explain himself. He liked keeping a mystery about things.

If Daly and Prine wanted to see what Stu Byner was bringing to town, then

154

they'd just have to damned well step outside and take a peek.

Prine heard wagon brakes creak outside in the street. Stu Byner jumped down off his seat right away and went around to the back of the wagon.

By this time, Prine and Daly were hurrying out the door and over to the wagon. Byner waited until the lawmen were beside him. He said, "It ain't pretty, Sheriff."

He pulled back a ratty red blanket he'd thrown over the body. There were a number of different ways they could have killed her. They'd chosen just about the worst. They'd cut her throat.

A lurid dark red snake of deep slashes and crusted scabbing stretched over three quarters of her neck. Her hands were mournful expressions of her last few moments — bloody gashes where the knife had cut them as she held them up for protection. He hadn't realized before, not until he'd seen it in the clear morning sunlight, just how elegant the bones of her face were. Or had been. Her blood-smeared and bruised cheeks were garish with death now.

She wore the white blouse and butternuts she'd worn last night. Her body was still dusty and dirty. She was bled white, as if a thousand leeches had been set upon her.

All Prine could think of was that he could have saved her life. He could have saved her life.

CHAPTER TWELVE

For an hour that morning, Daly, Carlyle, and Prine lived in another dimension. The dimension of anxious waiting. They stayed inside the sheriff's office, not wanting to go out and answer questions the crowd was sure to ask. They drank coffee and smoked and didn't say much to each other. They dreaded what lay ahead.

A horseman had been dispatched to Neville's place. He carried a note from the sheriff informing him of the death of his sister and informing Neville that the three lawmen were waiting for him at the sheriff's office.

"Wonder how he'll be," Carlyle said.

"You can't ever tell with him," Daly said. "Time somebody burned down his barn, he got so angry I thought he was going to have a heart attack. Wouldn't take any help from me or anybody else. Not even his own men. Went after the man himself. And caught him, too. Brought him back thrown over a horse. Went to the county attorney personally and made sure the man got the maximum penalty the county attorney could put on him."

"But then there was the other time when somebody robbed his old man on the stage road," Carlyle said. "You imagine that, Tom? Havin' the brass to rob old man Neville himself? He was all alone in his buggy and headed home, and this punk came out of nowhere and robbed him. Took everything but his britches. And young Neville stayed so calm, I thought somethin' was wrong with him."

"You're forgettin' the other end of that story," Daly said.

"Oh? What other end?"

"The punk goes to prison, and he's in there maybe two weeks when he gets into it with this other convict. Guy beats him to death with his fists. But guess what? They find a knife on the punk, and the convict says that the punk attacked him and he was only actin' in self-defense. I talked to the warden a couple years later, and he said he knew damned good and well that the knife had been planted on the punk after he was dead but that he couldn't do anything about it. All the cons, they stuck up for the killer. The warden said that he learned later that every man in that partic- ular cell block had gotten twenty dollars to go along with the story about the punk havin' the knife. And guess who put up the money? The warden couldn't prove that, either, but he said it was Richard Neville for sure."

Then Daly and Carlyle fell to speculating about how many men would be with Neville when he came to town. They seemed to agree that he would bring most of his ranch hands. They knew the terrain. They were good shots. And Neville was sure to keep them keen with the promise of a large reward for the two, dead or alive.

Prine took it all in. Listening, assessing. Had Cassie told Tolan and Rooney that Tom had been there and wanted to take her back? If she had, then they would surely tell Neville this when they were captured. And then the questions would be asked about why Tom hadn't brought her back. He'd have to tell Daly and Neville the truth — that she was part of it. And he would have to make a convincing case for himself — that he'd been out looking for her when he happened to see a lantern flash in the abandoned farmhouse. And that she wouldn't come back to town with him. But how would he explain that he hadn't gone straight to Daly when he'd come back to town? There was only one way. To protect Cassie, he had to let the faked kidnapping play out.

Would Neville believe him? Would Neville hold him responsible for her death? Would Neville have him taken care of the way he'd had the punk in prison taken care of?

Daly and Carlyle went on talking about the various reactions Richard Neville had had to bad moments in his life. One thing became clear. You didn't defeat Richard Neville. Never. He had the intelligence and the money and the time to find you and crush you. He also had the will to do it.

Prine cursed his damned dumb dream. . . .

Why hadn't he stuck with Lucy? Why did he always have to be so big and important in his own mind? Why did he have to prove and prove and prove again that he really was this important man?

Fear. Fear and confusion. And all because he'd had this damned dumb dream of marrying a rich girl and launching himself on a lifetime of gentried pleasure.

Fear and confusion. He felt young and foolish; and yet he also felt old and mean and smart enough to know that he would take great satisfaction in killing Tolan and Rooney when he finally caught up with them.

★ ★ ★

A lone horse and rider came into town just before noon. The rider didn't seem to be in any particular hurry.

The first man to see the rider jumped up on the sidewalk in front of the sheriff's office and started pounding. "He's here! He's here, Sheriff!"

By this time, most of the crowd had dispersed, gone back to their lives. But there were always a few stragglers who found the lives of others — particularly if they involved tragedy — far more interesting than their own.

None of the lawmen went out to greet Neville. Daly figured he'd resent them pouncing on him. Let him take his own time walking in.

They could hear him tying his horse to the hitching post outside, hear him on the sidewalk, hear him pushing open the front door, the hinges of which had developed a faint squeak in the past few days.

The dark suit. The white shirt. The black hat. Standard attire for Richard Neville. But the two Colts strapped gunnywise across his hips weren't standard at all. Nor was the harsh, cold look of the face. The eyes that had always reflected his slight air of superiority now reflected

161

nothing the three men had ever seen before. Whatever it was, it fitted with the
guns he wore.

He offered no greeting. He said,
"Where's my sister's body, Sheriff?"

"Over at the mortuary."

"I figured. Somebody from the ranch
will be in this afternoon to make arrange-
ments. He'll also tell the monsignor what
we want."

"We're all sorry about this, Richard."

"That's fine. I know you're sincere. And
I appreciate it. But it doesn't help what I
feel inside."

"We've got a pretty good idea who they
are."

"I've got a better idea than that, Sheriff.
The ranch hand who was with Cassie when
they kidnapped her spotted them in town
yesterday. Recognized one of them and
then started asking about them. Tolan and
Rooney are their names."

"That's who we're looking for, too,
Richard. Tolan and Rooney. I was waiting
for you to get here so you could lead part
of the posse if you wanted to."

Neville set his black-gloved hands on the
handles of his Colts. "No posse, Sheriff.
This is something for just a couple of men.
Knowing their kind, they're holed up

somewhere drinking. Whoring. They didn't get the money they wanted, and now they're wanted for murder. So they're going to be scared, too. All that plays just right for us."

"You sure you don't want a posse, Richard?"

Neville looked at Prine. "I just want your deputy to ride with me. He's a good shot, and he knew Cassie slightly. That gives him a little bit of a stake in this. That all right with you, Prine?"

Prine, in his state of mind — fear and confusion — wondered if Neville knew about his role in the kidnapping. Not reporting it, then Cassie dying — what if he knew? What if this was a trap of some kind? But he quickly answered, "Sure. I'll leave whenever you want to."

"Let's go right now."

"Get yourself some extra rifle rounds," Daly said. He obviously didn't approve of Neville's plans, but he wasn't about to try and stop the man. His sister had been killed. He had first dibs on how they went after her killers. Plus — and there was always this plus with the Neville family — he was the most powerful man in this area of the state.

Prine got himself ready. He dug out his

Bowie knife and scabbard, his field glasses, and his saddle roll. He took thirty extra Winchester rounds.

"In case we don't run up against them," Neville said as Prine was gathering up his extra gear, "you tell the newspaper to print up a hundred fliers saying there's a twenty-five-thousand-dollar reward for anybody who brings them in dead or alive. But I think you know the way I'd prefer them to come back to town."

"I sure do, Richard," Daly, ever the Neville enthusiast, said. "I sure do."

Prine went out and got his horse ready and his canteen filled, then spoke to a couple of deadbeats who still hadn't sucked enough excitement from the fruit of this wonderful moment when a beautiful rich girl went and got herself killed.

Neville came out then. The deadbeats asked him something Prine didn't hear. Neville didn't try and placate them at all. He just scowled at them and brought his horse around with such force that the deadbeats were forced to jump out of the way.

He said absolutely nothing to Prine. He just galloped away and expected Prine to catch up.

CHAPTER THIRTEEN

They rode toward the sun.

The land was a patchwork of changing topography. They rode through a long, wide stand of timber that had been divided down the center to create a road. They forged a river wild from recent rains. They traveled a stretch of desertlike land where the only things that seemed to bloom were timid-looking cactus and scruffy gray plants. Always, the distant mountains rose to the sky to their right. After two that afternoon, the temperature began to fall. Rain clouds with spider legs could be seen in the distance. It wouldn't be long before they'd get the rain and probably lose the tracks they were following.

The first place they'd stopped was the deserted farmhouse where Cassie had been kept. They'd found that two horses had headed toward the sun. They also found that the shoes on one of the horses had been put on at an odd angle, making it reasonably easy to keep track of.

Most of the time they didn't talk much.

A few times Prine heard Neville muttering to himself. Probably the rage got to be so much he had to express it. This was a very different Neville than the glad-hander he'd met at the mansion the other night. He felt sorry for this Neville, and ashamed that he hadn't done his duty as a lawman.

The rain started midafternoon. They continued to follow the tracks as far as they could, finally cresting a hill that overlooked a stage station.

"Looks like they might have stopped down there," Prine said. "I wonder why."

"Let's go find out."

Thunder rippled across the sky and a slash of lightning cast everything into a hellish, colorless relief that made the tracks they were following almost grotesquely dark. The devil would leave such tracks.

The stage station wasn't as bad as some. The barns and stables that held fresh animals and supplies looked well-kept and cleaned. The front yard wasn't a field of animal shit. It had been raked, and you could see that grass was trying very hard to pop up here and there. You could almost hear it straining.

They knew what awaited them if they stayed here. The food would run to tainted bacon and hard biscuits and water just starting to go bad. That was the usual repast, anyway.

They were lucky. The rain came smashing down, beads of hail and all, three or four minutes after they entered the sod-roofed stage station.

The layout was typical. Fireplace, three large, picnic-style tables, an open area for males to sleep on at night. Far in the corner was an extra-large bed where the station manager's wife slept, usually with a few of the female guests. The dirt floor didn't look like a barnyard, and the food smells surprised them. Some kind of stew bubbling in a pot.

From the outbuildings came the shouts of the station manager's three kids. They'd been battening everything down, given the ferocity of the rain.

The station man turned out to look like a parson — tall, grave, and disapproving of everything that passed before his eyes. He was probably thirty and looked sixty. His bald and gleaming scalp didn't help. Nor did his severe mouth and pinched eyes. He offered neither a hand nor a greeting.

"You didn't come in on the stage," he said.

"Good guess," Prine said. "You were standing out there watching us come in."

"We're waiting for a stage now. There won't be any room for extras tonight."

"We're not looking to be put up for the night," Neville said. "We're looking for two men."

A woman came through the doorway. She was soaked. She bent over and wrung her dark hair out with strong but nicely shaped hands. When she looked up, they saw her face. She was everything her husband was not. She actually smiled at them.

Her husband said, "I told them there's no room."

She spoke in a joshing way. "Frank's getting old. He forgets things. There's plenty of room in the barn, if you don't mind the loft."

"We won't be needing a place if the rain lets up," Prine said. "What we want is some information."

"Well," she said, elbowing old Frank in the ribs, "you came to the wrong place. Frank wouldn't tell you the time of day if you gave him the watch. He don't cotton much to strangers."

"Seems like he's in the right business," Prine said.

She smiled. "I'm Beth, by the way." She glanced impishly at her husband. "That's the way you have to talk to Frank. Make

168

fun of him a little. God knows he deserves it, don't you, Frank?"

And then the damnedest thing happened. The hard face of Ichabod started reluctantly — very reluctantly — breaking into a tiny smile. Tiny, tiny, the way a kid will smile against his will when you start to tickle him.

"Damned women," he said, and then stalked out the front door and angled off, disappearing, presumably, for the barn or one of the other outbuildings.

She said, "He gets jealous. Sees two gents like you — nice-looking and nice manners and you with that badge — he always thinks I'm gonna leave him. That's what happened to his first wife. Up and left him for a traveling salesman. Took their only kid and he's never seen either of them again. I guess I wouldn't trust nobody either, somethin' like that happened to me. I better go talk to him. Settle him down some."

"Guess we may as well wait out the storm," Prine said.

"I hate to lose the time."

"We'll have a hard time finding their tracks in a downpour like this."

Neville's jaw muscles started to work. "Guess you're right."

Kerosene lanterns played chase with the shadows in the large, rectangular room.

They ate a passable supper of fried potatoes and beans. The stage arrived just as they were finishing up. The two men sat in the corner watching the people straggle in. The rain was finally letting up. The stage passengers settled in for the night. The driver was soaked and had to borrow clothes from Frank Barstow. You could hear that he already had a bad head cold. By morning it would probably move down into his chest.

The two gunnies didn't come until the rain was little more than a mist. Prine and Neville were already in their bedroll over in the corner. Most of the passengers were still at the tables, talking, though by now the words had gotten muffled from drowsiness. The majority of them would be asleep within half an hour.

Neville had the back of his hand over his eyes. He wasn't trying to sleep. Just rest.

"Bogstad and Case," Prine whispered to him.

"What?" Neville said.

Prine leaned down on an elbow and spoke softly. "I saw those two in town one day talking to Tolan. I got curious about

170

them. They're gunnies and bounty hunters, it turns out."

"You think they had anything to do with the kidnapping?" Neville started to sit up, but Prine pushed him back down.

"Let's see what they're doing here. I doubt they had anything to do with the killing, or they wouldn't be around this close to town. But let's see why they're here."

Bogstad and Case were loud and insulting. They complained about the coffee, the food, the fire not being built up, and the lack of good-looking women on the stage. One of the male passengers spoke up in defense of his female traveling partners, but Case just told him to shut up or he'd be sorry.

They were wet and cold, they said, otherwise they'd leave this little hellhole. They looked like brothers — short, heavy, grimy, in need of a shave, a bath, and more than a little redemption. Prine had run dozens of men like Bogstad and Case into jail dozens of times. They just couldn't stand to see a peaceful situation, people getting along, enjoying themselves. Their pleasure was other people's misery. And they damned well made people miserable, too, threatening them, insulting them, humiliating them. They were especially good at embarrassing a man in front of his woman.

And that's where they got to around nine o'clock that night.

Frank and Beth sat at one of the tables with the passengers. They were talking about the forthcoming senatorial election. Everybody agreed that both men made pretty bad candidates.

Bogstad came up behind Beth and said, "I'd like the pleasure of this dance, lady."

She stayed sweet. "But there isn't any music."

"Don't need music. Now, stand up."

"I'd prefer to sit here with my husband and our guests."

Bogstad looked back at his partner and said, "She won't dance with me, Case. What should I do?"

"Kill her." He laughed.

"That sounds about right," Bogstad said.

An old woman at the table said, "We were having a nice conversation."

"Well, excuse me all to hell, old lady. But I want to dance with this here gal."

Bogstad had apparently assumed that nobody at the table would present him with any problem. Frank Barstow surprised everybody, maybe even himself.

Barstow brought up an early-model Colt that looked to weigh twenty-eight pounds. There were a lot better updated Colts on the market, but this one would do just fine, thank you. This close to his target, Barstow could put a considerable hole in Bogstad's chest.

"You and your friend git now. And I mean now."

Bogstad grinned. "You shouldn't ever threaten a man when your hand is shakin' like that."

Prine saw what was going to happen and decided to step in. The first thing he did was stand up and quickly cross over to the chair where Case was sitting. Case was ready to draw when he thought he was needed. Prine showed him his badge and forced him to turn over both his gun and his Bowie knife.

Neville was up, too. He walked over to Bogstad and said, "Put the gun down. Your partner's covered. Nobody here to help you. Put the gun down and walk out of here, just as Mr. Barstow said. You understand?"

Bogstad wasn't a man of pride. He wouldn't fight on principle when he was outnumbered. He'd surrender his gun and his person, knowing that if you didn't kill Prine and Neville now, he would someday, some way have an opportunity to shoot them in the back and overtake them with a band of gunnies like himself. Patience was every bit as much a weapon as a six-gun. Prine always laughed at the dime-novel gunfights when they faced off many yards apart. Most gunfights involved the front of a pistol and the back of a human. Or an assassin in shadow. Most gunfighters were like Bogstad here. Cowards with Colts.

Bogstad handed his weapon to Prine. "Now, don't you go sellin' that on me. My ma gave me that for my third birthday." Since he didn't get a laugh, he said, "You're Prine. That deputy from Claybank. Maybe you should know that me 'n' Case over there're on the same side you are."

He turned around, faced Prine.

"Yeah, how's that?"

"We're after Tolan and Rooney, too. We don't think it's right that the pretty young gal shoulda been done that way."

"Of course, this wouldn't have anything to do with the reward, now, would it?"

Bogstad snorted. "Now, just because I don't look too good or smell too good or talk too good, don't mean I don't care about my fellow human beings."

"Where'd you get a line like that?"

"Theater," Case said from the back of the room. He pronounced it "thee-ater." "Outside Kansas City. We was laughin' for days about it. Funniest daggone line I ever heard me."

Prine ignored him. "You have any idea where Tolan and Rooney are?"

Bogstad said, "Now, why would you think that?"

"Because I saw you talking to them at least twice in Claybank. Right before the kidnapping."

"We know 'em, sure," Bogstad said.

"From where?"

"Here and there. Around."

"That isn't very specific."

"We're sort of in the same line of work, you might say."

"But you wouldn't happen to know where they might have headed?"

"We got just about as much information as you do, Deputy."

Prine drove his fist hard into Bogstad's stomach.

Bogstad doubled over. He looked shocked as well as pained. "What the hell was that for?"

"For interrupting these people. They were just having a nice time, and you had to ruin it for them."

He picked up Bogstad's six-shooter and emptied it of bullets, which he set on the table. "Now you and your partner get out of here, the way Mr. Barstow said." He handed Bogstad his empty gun.

Bogstad walked with some difficulty. He still couldn't stand up quite straight. The pain in his stomach was obviously still severe. He went to the door, and Case joined him there. Case preceded Bogstad outside.

Neville came up. "You're just letting them walk away? They may know something."

"I'm sure they do," Prine said. "And that's why we're going to follow them."

Chapter Fourteen

Bogstad and Case took the route Prine had assumed they would. A town named Picaro lay twenty miles due north of here. It was the remnants of a boomtown notorious even among boomtowns for its violence and corruption. It was still innocent of any real law, so it would be a good place for two men on the run to put up for a while.

They climbed into the foothills again, the terrain rougher now, rocky on the one hand, muddy on the other. Bogstad and Case didn't make good time, nor did Prine and Neville.

When they were able to ride side by side, Neville said, "I didn't treat her very well."

"You did what you could. Raising a kid when you're a kid isn't easy."

"She always said I didn't take her seriously, and now that I think about it, I think she was right. I just keep thinking of all the ways I could've treated her better. I was a piss-poor brother."

Prine knew there was no point in arguing, trying to make Neville feel better.

Dawn was turning out the stars. Pumas and wild dogs and wolves were waking, making growling morning noises, padding about their immediate areas searching for food. Best to listen to their voices and forget Neville. He was at the stage in his grieving where he had to be honest with himself, had to admit that the way he'd handled his sister had been wrong. She'd been more nuisance than sister to him, something he needed to control because it would look bad for his peacock ego if he didn't. Prine knew what he was going through. Prine was going through something of the same thing. He'd learned a lot about himself last night. Learned that his dreams of wealth and prominence were the dreams of a child, not of an adult. Maybe he could've saved Cassie's life if he hadn't been so foolish; and maybe he wouldn't have had to break Lucy's heart because he was so selfish.

"She thought a lot of you," Prine said, giving in. That's what Neville wanted to hear, and what the hell — who did it hurt to lie in this way?

"When did she tell you that?"

"The other night. After the recital."

"You're not bullshitting me?"

"Why would I bullshit you? That's what she said."

"Why was she talking about me?"

Prine shrugged. "Just talking about her life. How much she liked working at the church. And thinking about her future. And how good to her you always were."

Neville spat. "That's the kind of shit I am, Prine. I push her around the way I did and she thinks I'm treating her decently. There's going to be a special place for me in hell, I can tell you that."

By full light, they could see Picaro below them. The town was girdled by deserted mines and large pieces of rusted mining equipment. There were so many failed mines just before the last recession that the equipment lost most of its value. Wasn't worth the shipping prices, given the minuscule profit the mine owners would make.

Through his field glasses, Prine could see that some of the equipment was already rusted clean through. The gear looked like giant steel animals, long dead.

The town itself looked decent enough. Several blocks of whitewashed little houses that had probably been owned by the mining company at one point. Couple churches, two long blocks of commercial buildings, a redbrick schoolhouse with an athletic field next to it, two factories, and some small stucco buildings that looked like manufacturing shops of some kind. For a town whose boom days were past, Picaro looked all right.

Neville was hiding in his silence again. Prine didn't mind. He was sleepy enough to slump in his saddle. Sometimes in the past few hours he'd felt unreal, as if he were witnessing all the events of the past thirty-six hours without participating. There was a deadness in him that precluded all feelings except fear.

He jerked awake at the outskirts of town. Some scruffy kids were splashing through the mud puddles in the road, screeching and hollering and giggling as they did so. He envied them. A pure perfect image came to him. He was eight and playing baseball with his brother in the front yard, and he had just hit a baseball farther than he ever had. And his brother, who'd never paid him much respect before — his brother's whole attitude changed right then and there. He never forgot it. His brother didn't push him around anymore. Call him names. Punish him. Prine still wasn't quite an equal, but he came damned close.

His poncho had started to dry off. He

was completely sweated inside it. If they didn't have any luck here, he'd push Neville to stay over for eight hours, get some sleep, go at it fresh again. You could bet that was what Tolan and Rooney would be doing — if not here, somewhere down the line.

They went straight for the sheriff's office. A tough-looking, middle-aged Mexican in a sombrero and a serape sat on a bench outside the stucco building. His outsize badge was easy to see on the serape. So was the sawed-off shotgun laid across his lap. He was rolling a cigarette and watching them ease up to the hitching post.

"Welcome to our town, gentlemen," he said. "I'm Sheriff Gomez." He smiled with bad teeth. "If you're wondering how a Mex got to be sheriff in a white man's town . . ." There was something obscene about his laugh. "It's because the gringos are too scared to be sheriff themselves."

He finished rolling the cigarette, set it between his lips, produced a lucifer from inside his serape, and ignited it with a thumbnail. "How may I be of service?"

"We're looking for two men," Prine said.

"Your badge — these must be bad men, no?" There was a sardonic tone to his words that Prine didn't like.

"Their names are Tolan and Rooney," Neville said. "They murdered my sister." He'd clearly picked up on Gomez's sarcastic tone, too — and didn't like it. "My name's Richard Neville. If you haven't heard of me, you've heard of my father. I would recommend that you don't give me or my friend here any shit. Because if you do, I'll tear that fucking sneer off your face and then cut your heart out. You understand, amigo?"

Neville's bitter words didn't have much effect on Gomez. "Then I should be impressed and cower in fear?"

"You should do your job," Prine snapped. "We're looking for two killers, and we need to know if they've passed through your town here."

The front door of the sheriff's office opened and a man, also Mexican, emerged. He was the opposite of the other man. Tall, trim, handsome, well-dressed in a business suit, he stepped into the daylight and said, "Good morning, gentlemen. I was waiting for my stupid deputy here to explain to you his joke. I'm Marshal Valdez. This despicable creature here is my brother-in-law, whose presence has been forced upon me by familial obligations."

Gomez didn't seem the least embarrassed by this revelation. In fact, he yawned, stretched, stood up, and said, "It is time for a hardworking man like me to have himself some breakfast."

"Remember what I told you about the whorehouse, Gomez," Valdez said. "If you get rough with any of the women next time you're drunk, I'll put you in jail for a week and take away your badge."

Gomez smirked. "Someday I will be wearing that badge. Then we shall see what we shall see." He made a pass at giving a bow but almost fell over on his face. For the first time, Prine realized the man was drunk. Gomez wandered off.

"Come inside, please," Marshal Valdez said, "and let me again apologize for the rudeness of Gomez. He lives inside a bottle."

The jailhouse was tidy, smelled clean, and was arranged into a front desk, two small offices in the rear, and four cells behind a locked door. The marshal's office was heavy with a large wooden desk, a bookcase filled with what appeared to be legal tomes, and a wall decorated with the minimal number of awards, citations, and photographs of the marshal shaking hands with people he obviously considered to be important. Prine didn't recognize any of them.

The marshal called out a name that seemed garbled — "Lucentia" was as close as Prine could get it — and two minutes later a fetching young girl of no more than eighteen appeared and blessed each man with a cup of steaming coffee. "My daughter, gentlemen. You can see why I am so proud of her."

The pretty girl was dressed in a white peasant blouse and skirt, looking more gypsy than Mexican. When she smiled, she also tried to speak. The sound made the back of Prine's neck freeze. She could not articulate the words she was trying to speak.

"That is our family shame," Marshal Valdez said in his formal, somewhat stiff way. "Three years ago we had some trouble here. A range war of sorts. The one side felt that I was too friendly with the other. They accused me, in fact, of being on the payroll of the other. A man in my position, he can't tolerate such slander, of course. So I myself — and my men, even Gomez — began riding against them. Since they insisted we were on the other side, then why not *be* on the other side. Of course, our friends were so happy to have

184

us fight with them that they insisted we take money. Some people to this day insist that it was a bribe so that they could have the law on their side. I have tried to explain that many times to many people — that our intentions were only good and true — but you know how cynical some people can be. They're always looking for the worst in other people."

This guy had a line of bullshit that stretched clear from here to Buffalo, New York, Prine thought. He had to give him one thing, though. He was a dazzler. He could hold an audience with the best of them.

"But you are no doubt wondering what any of this has to do with my lovely daughter Lucretia. Too simple — and too tragic. They broke into our house one night. I am a widower. Lucretia was home alone. They cut her tongue out. Later, one of the men who helped to do this terrible thing, he told me that this would be worse than killing her. Because every time I looked at my daughter now, I would see what selling my badge had done. That was how the gentleman put it. 'Selling my badge.' I myself personally castrated him. I made sure that he remained conscious. Then I poured kerosene upon him and set him on fire. I did not do this to please my men. Or to appease some crowd of lowborns. I did it to avenge my daughter. I did this alone, with no one else around to see. I waited till he was nothing more than ash and bone, and then I threw him into a pit of rattlers I kept in the ground behind the jail. Sometimes prisoners do not want to talk. Showing them the snake pit can be a very effective means of making them more cooperative." He nodded to Lucretia. "This, then, is my tragic daughter."

The girl looked curiously angry as he told this story. Prine figured it must be having to relive the terrible events that led to her being mute. She'd probably appreciate it if her father wasn't always bringing it up. He'd be pissed off every time he thought of it. The girl curtsied and left the office.

Valdez got up and poured brandy from a fancy cut-glass bottle. Each cup got a strong dose of it. "The coffee is not to every palate. Jail coffee, what can you expect? The brandy is the best one can buy. It makes even this coffee bearable." Finished serving, he capped the bottle and sat down again.

"Now, gentlemen," said the splendid — just ask him — Mexican, "how is it I may serve you?"

"We're looking for two men. Tolan and Rooney are their names," Prine said.

"These are bad men?"

"Very bad men. They kidnapped Mr. Neville's sister and then murdered her."

Valdez was so dramatic in response to this news that he looked as though he might purely faint. "An outrage against all that is true and holy."

"They came this way," Prine said. "They may be in Picaro now."

The drama continued. The fabulous Mexican put his hand on his fist and shook his noble head. "It is a wonder that God above does not strike us all dead, the things we do to each other."

Prine was starting to feel faint from all the ham acting. He said, "We need your permission to look around town. We're not asking for anything official. We just want to check the hotels and the saloons, mostly."

"You do not want to use my men?"

"We don't want to signal them we're here. If your men start asking questions, it won't be long before they figure out that we're here looking for them."

"I see. A point well taken, my friend. But in such a heinous matter — I will be most cooperative in any way you suggest. And if these two should end up in my jail, I can assure you they will rot there."

Neville spoke for the first time. "We'll take them back with us to Claybank."

"Of course, whatever you wish. Cooperation is what I promised you, and cooperation is what you shall have."

Prine said, "We're pretty tired, but we're going to start looking for them right away. Then we'll get some sleep and some grub."

"Your poor sister," Valdez said. "She was young, Mr. Neville?"

"Twenty-three."

"A child — an innocent flower. These men will pay for what they've done, believe me."

"Thank you, Marshal," Neville said. "Now we need to get going."

Prine and Neville pushed up from their chairs. The brandy had made Prine groggy. He needed cold wind to cut his lethargy.

A man in a white apron over Levi's and a red wool shirt walked past the door, nodding. "Good morning, Marshal. This food is much better than they deserve."

It stood to reason that since everything else was so splendid about Marshal Valdez, his laugh would be splendid, too. On stage, it would carry well to all the highest seats in the balcony. Valdez the opera star.

"You say that every morning, Mr. Wiley."

"I say it because it's that good every morning."

Prine had the feeling that the banter was part of an entire ritual. A really boring one.

Wiley vanished. Prine heard the heavy door leading to the cells in back being opened and then closed. There would likely be a slot for food trays built into the cell doors.

"Remember, my friends, I will take every opportunity to help you."

Prine glanced at Neville. Neville looked as weary of this splendiferous speech as Prine was.

Prine thought they'd walk themselves to the front door. But Valdez couldn't just let them go, could he? What kind of host would he be?

"This is a lovely town, this Picaro," he said, escorting them up front. "I hope you have time to enjoy the cultural activities."

Whorehouses, gambling pits, maybe a hoedown or two. Those would be the cultural activities, Prine reasoned. Valdez here could make a good living writing brochures for tourists. With his grandiose manner of speech, he could make a pigsty sound like a Bavarian castle.

Then, at last, they were outside and Valdez was closing the door behind them.

"That guy's as full of shit as a Christmas turkey," Neville said.

"You trust him?"

"Do you?"

"Fuck no," Prine said.

"He's angling for something, but I'm not sure what."

"Money. I'm just trying to figure out how he's going to get it out of us."

"You think he knows where they are?"

"Probably. But there isn't anything we can do about it. He's got jurisdiction here. He's paying me the courtesy of asking around for Tolan and Rooney. But he doesn't even have to do that if he doesn't want to."

"Your badge doesn't travel?"

"Not outside the limits of Claybank county, it doesn't. And we're a long ways from Clayback county."

"A long ways," Neville said, looking around at the town. "A long ways."

CHAPTER FIFTEEN

There were five saloons, if you counted a private club called The Gentleman's Grill. They split them up and set about their work.

The first one Prine entered was a latrine with walls and a roof. He didn't know what he was smelling, but whatever it was was long dead. Not that the customers seemed to notice in the crypt-shadowy place that consisted of a raw timber bar and three long benches along the east wall. The place wasn't ten feet wide. A dog was noisily eating something from the damp dirt floor. Prine wouldn't have been surprised if the meal consisted of a human corpse.

One drunk had his head down on the bar. Passing out while you were standing was no modest feat. Another drunk, one of those sitting on the bench, had puked on himself but didn't seem to notice. He was conversing with another drunk who kept almost sliding off the bench. There was another drunk who every few seconds would raise his head and shout, "I need some pussy over here!"

The bartender was ridiculously dapper, a merry fop in a leper colony. White shirt, string tie, rimless glasses, hard dead smile, white hair. He had to be in his late sixties.

"Is that a real badge?" he said.

"It is if you live in Claybank."

"You're a ways away from home."

"Your marshal was telling me about all the cultural activities in town here." He looked around. "I thought I'd check one of them out."

"Believe me, mister," the bartender said, "you can't insult this place. All the jokes have been told. And as for the marshal, we pay that sonofabitch through the nose to stay in business here. He makes as much from this place as I do."

"That doesn't surprise me."

"Oh? Claybank pretty clean, is it?"

"The sheriff doesn't get a cut from the saloons or the whorehouses, if that's what you mean."

"Maybe I'll move there."

"And leave a nice place like this?"

Just then, the drunk who'd thrown up on himself threw up on himself again.

"He'll clean himself up later," the bartender said. "He'll wobble down to the river and throw himself in."

"Lucky river."

Three drunks came in the front door, arguing about some horse race. There seemed to be an unwritten law operating here. Not until you'd almost reached the blackout stage of drunkenness were you allowed to enter this hallowed land.

"So what can I do you for, Deputy? I've got customers to take care of."

"Take care of them and come back."

A few minutes later, the bartender appeared out of the murk at the far end of the bar and said, "So how can I help you?"

Prine told him and the man said instantly, "Yeah, they were here."

"When?"

"Last night."

"You happen to know if they're still around?"

"Now, how the hell would I know that?"

"So you haven't seen 'em around anywhere today?"

"Not today."

"They do anything in particular last night?"

"Drank. Kept to themselves. Left, I dunno, maybe eleven o'clock. If I hadn't been serving them beers, I wouldn't have known they were here."

"They talk to anybody here?"

"Not that I saw. They didn't look real

friendly. And the big one kept his Bowie knife on the table, like he just might be of a mind to use it all of a sudden."

"You see anybody here now who was in here last night?"

The bartender glanced around. "Murphy over there. Redhead with the long red beard. He was in here for a while last night."

"You see them again, I'll be staying at the Fordham Hotel. Name's Prine. Tom Prine."

The bartender nodded. Didn't say goodbye.

The redhead was talking to himself, which Prine assumed was not a good sign. Sitting up front all by himself on a stretch of bench. Just jabbering away. He apparently thought he was pretty funny, because every thirty seconds or so he'd laugh hard at something he'd just said.

He was probably forty. He had beggar-sad eyes and no teeth. His smell could repel bullets. Up close, Prine saw that the man hadn't been laughing. He'd been crying. His blue eyes were wet and his lower lip had Saint Vitus' dance. He had a violent tic that twisted his neck half around every few minutes.

Prine said, "Bartender tells me you were in here late last night."

Murphy looked at Prine's badge. "I wasn't lookin' in no windows this time. I honest wasn't. The priest, he tole me not to look at no more naked women through their windows. He said I scairt them when I did. So I ain't done it no more."

When he spoke, he pushed the stench of his breath farther and wider than it would normally travel. Prine stepped back from him.

"There were two men in here last night. Tolan and Rooney. You remember them?"

"They say something agin me?" Murphy, agitated, said. "People always say things again me and they got no right, no right."

"Did they buy you drinks? Two men? Last night?"

"I stay away from them windas now. And I don't look at naked ladies, either. I swear to God I don't."

Prine grabbed the man by the shoulder, squeezed. The old man's eyes reflected sudden pain.

"Last night. You were talking with two men. Tolan and Rooney."

The expression shifted. A half-smile of recognition. "Oh, yes, them two. They was mostly makin' fun of ole Murphy, was what they was doin'. But they kept buyin' me drinks, so I put up with 'em."

Prine squeezed harder. Tears gleamed in the old man's eyes again. "I want you to think hard now."

"It hurts awful, mister. It hurts awful."

"Just answer my questions."

"It hurts awful. Just awful."

"Did they say anything about where they were going?"

"Going?"

"After they left the saloon."

"Bad place," the old man said, and then started babbling to himself again. "They kick ole Murphy out. Say I was tryin' to peek in the doors and see the naked women. But I just wanted warm to see. I needed warm. The snow and cold. Murphy needed warm was all. Sonsofbitches, dirty sonsofbitches." He made a pathetic little fist.

"The bad place? Where's that, Murphy?"

Looking at Prine as if for the first time, Murphy said, "You work for them, don't you?"

"Work for who, Murphy?"

"I shoulda seen that right off. You work for them. You was there the night they drove me out in the cold and Murphy got pneumonia and damn near died. You was one of them that run me off, wasn't you?"

"Where is this bad place, Murphy?"

"You know where it is."

"No, I don't, Murphy. I really don't."

A drunk four feet away said, "You talkin' about the bad place again, Murphy?"

"You just shut up," Murphy said. "You just shut up."

"He means the Empire Hotel," the other drunk said. He was a man of hair so wild, he looked like an insane jungle beast of some kind. "They kicked him out one winter night when they caught him sleepin' in one of the rooms. He was sick — pneumonia, like he said — and they run him out of there and he got a lot sicker by mornin'. The doc damned near couldn't save his life. About five times a day, ole Murph here remembers it and gets mad all over again."

"This Empire Hotel still in business?"

"Right down at the end of the next block."

"I'm gonna blow that place up some night," Murphy said as Prine was leaving. He was still talking to himself. "You wait and see. Ole Murphy'll blow it up one of these days and they'll be sorry they ever treated me like that. Sorry to the end of their born days."

The Empire was a two-story Victorian-fronted place with a colored man in some kind of smart wine-red uniform just inside the vestibule to take your luggage. Drummers, judging by all the checkered suits and heavy valises, preferred this particular hotel when in the embrace of Picaro. The colored man looked sad when he saw that Prine had no bags.

Prine went up to the desk, where a middle-aged woman in a bun and a severe gaze said, "Help you, cowboy?" She apparently didn't notice his badge.

"I'm looking for two men who might be staying here."

"We have forty-seven guests at the moment. You'll have to help me out there. Oh, a badge, huh?"

"You can check me out with Marshal Valdez if you'd like."

Icy smile. "I can tell you aren't from around here."

"Why's that?"

"Why's that? Because he won't talk unless you pay him to, and even then he lies most of the time anyway. You over to his office, were you?"

"Yeah."

"His daughter? With her tongue cut out?"

"She's a beautiful girl."

"He sing you his sad song about these

198

terrible men cutting her tongue out as a way of getting back at him?"

"It is a sad song, ma'am. You shouldn't make fun of it."

"It'd be sad if it was true. Hell, he raped her himself and then cut her tongue out and made up this story to tell his wife. But the girl wrote her mother a letter, explaining everything. Then the mother died in a drowning that the coroner always said looked funny to him. You know what 'funny' means, don't you, son?"

"That he doesn't think she really drowned? That she was probably murdered?"

"That's exactly what he meant. But with her gone, and the note the daughter wrote missing, how's anybody gonna prove anything? But everybody knows the truth anyway. You got to watch yourself with Valdez, believe me."

Picaro was proving to be just the kind of place Prine had been searching for — the sort of town where a fella could settle down with a wife and raise some kids. And then hide out in the barn when all the local lunatics and degenerates came for you carrying torches and pitchforks.

He had no doubt that this version of the tongueless daughter was the true one. But he wondered what sinister secrets of her own this woman harbored.

He gave her the description of Tolan and Rooney.

"Oh," she said, "those two."

"They're here?" He sounded eager, too eager.

"Upstairs. They got pretty drunk last night." Then:

"What the Sam Hill is this?"

Marching through the front door, fanning out in military fashion, were six men carrying rifles. The leader was Gomez, the man who'd tried to pass himself off as the marshal of the town.

Gomez appeared to be much more sober than the last time Prine had seen him. He didn't wobble when he walked. And his gaze was fixed on the desk clerk as he stalked over to her, the barrel of his Winchester leading the way.

"There are two men here, Tolan and Rooney. Which room?"

She told them.

"They are there now?"

"As far as I know they are, Gomez."

"My name is Deputy Gomez. This would be a healthy thing for you to remember, senora."

The woman looked about to laugh, but

then stopped herself. "All right, Deputy Gomez, if that's the way you prefer it. Just remember, Marshal Valdez always gives me a little bit of the cut."

Gomez glanced at Prine and then back at the woman: "This so-called cut, I have no idea of what you're saying. We run this law and order here. We do not have 'cuts.' Cuts are for criminals and lawmen who do not honor their laws." This seemed to be for Prine's benefit, this profoundly moving and convincing speech on law and order. Prine was surprised that Gomez didn't choke on words as hypocritical as these.

Gomez angled his head to his men. "Let's go." To the desk clerk: "Do not try to warn them in any way, senora, as that would be bad for the health of your entire family."

Prine watched all the men but one go up the staircase. The lone man detached himself at the last moment and hurried down a long, narrow hall to the back. He'd cover the door opening on the alley.

"Looks like your friend Valdez beat you to it," the woman said.

"He's arresting them?" Prine said.

"In a way." A smile old and weary. "He obviously thinks they have money. He never arrests anybody who doesn't. He'll put them in a jail and then the local judge will set bail for some exorbitant price — which means any amount they can find on the men and in their room — and then the men will agree to pay this 'bail.' Then Valdez will give them half an hour to get out of town. If they try and come back, his men are told to kill them on sight."

"Bastard."

"You're right about that. Look what he did to his wife and daughter."

"There's never been a state official to look into all this?"

"What would they look into? The judge has a good standing with the state court and he's free to set any bail he wants. If the men go to court in his jurisdiction, they'll be found guilty because Valdez and the judge will have planted evidence that proves their guilt. So they won't take the chance of going to court. They just ride off and never come back here."

Prine explained about the kidnapping. "Valdez is going to be disappointed. He seems to think they have the ransom money. But they didn't get any. Those two probably don't have the price of a meal between them."

Shouts. A single gunshot. Thuds. And then the shouts were much louder, the men

202

out of the room and into the hallway now.

Tolan made a dramatic entrance. Somebody threw him down the stairs. He landed, badly bleeding head and all, on the floor directly across from Prine.

Rooney came down in handcuffs. There wasn't any blood, just looks of confusion and fear as Gomez kept jamming the barrel of his rifle into Rooney's back.

Tolan was grabbed and put on his feet and shoved across the open expanse in front of the door. Then he was pushed outside. Rooney, saying nothing, was shoved out right behind him.

By now, the hotel lobby was filled with drummers. There was an air of a convention about it, most of them holding brews from the hotel saloon and commenting with jokes and smirks about the two loudmouths who'd disrupted the air of camaraderie that normally existed in the hotel saloon. Last night apparently, Tolan had taken the liberty of moving several noses over a few inches.

Prine pushed his way through the crowd and left the hotel.

He found Neville on the sidewalk across from the sheriff's office. The time was pushing on toward noon. Vehicle traffic was steady. In the distance between the hotel and the jail you could see small groups of people who'd stood watching Tolan and Rooney being dragged off to imprisonment. It wasn't quite as good as a Fourth of July parade, but what the hell. It was better than watching wagons passing by and various horses and mules dropping road apples for the gourmet tastes of the local fly population.

"They just went inside," Neville said.

"Took them from the Empire Hotel."

"I wish I'd had a rifle. I could've taken care of them right now. Well, maybe on the trip back. I hate to see a man in handcuffs, but I'll make an exception in their case."

"I'm not sure it's going to be that easy to get them away from Valdez."

Neville sounded surprised. "Why the hell not? They killed my sister. You're a sworn deputy. Why the hell shouldn't we take them back? I'll tell you, Prine, I don't plan to take any shit from Valdez."

"We may have to."

"And why's that exactly?"

"Because," Prine said, "he's the local law and he's got the prisoners. We'll just have to go see him and see how this plays out."

"What the hell ever happened to law and order?"

Prine smiled. "A lot of people've been asking that question lately." He shrugged. "May as well get some lunch."

"Lunch? Let's go talk to Valdez."

"He'll want to talk to Tolan and Rooney first. Figure out what he wants to do with them."

"This doesn't make any sense. They're killers."

"C'mon. We could both use some grub."

Neville ate more than Prine would have imagined. A steak, two baked potatoes, two helpings of peas, and a large slice of pumpkin pie. Prine had the steak and a piece of bread and no pie. Despite his youth, he was getting a little puffy in the belly. He wanted to be ready when he got rich and famous. No reason a millionaire shouldn't look strong and slim. Of course, he wasn't exactly sure when that millionaire day would roll around. It seemed to be on a calendar that wouldn't be printed for a long, long time.

"So we go in and just take them," Neville said.

"He's the law, as I said. And he's got us outgunned."

"Then we threaten him."

"With what?"

"With my money and my status. I'm an

important man. I know that sounds like hell, but it's true. I want my sister's killers, and I'll use everything at hand to get them."

Prine had been going to say this. Now seemed an appropriate time. "If and when we get them, I'm in charge. And there won't be any killing. We take them back alive."

"A lot of things can happen on the trail."

"A lot of things," Prine said, "better *not* happen on the trail."

"I thought we were on the same side."

"We are. As long as you remember that I'm the law. And I don't mean the Valdez kind of law, either. I mean the Wyn Daly kind of law."

Neville smiled. It wasn't a pleasant smile. "I guess you aren't aware of all the favors Daly does for my crowd."

"I'm aware."

"And you still think he's such a great lawman."

"I didn't say he was great. I said he followed the law. Ninety-five percent of the time, anyway."

That smile again. Neville had reverted to the man Prine had met at the recital the other night. Arrogant, superior. "He follows the law unless you're rich. And then

206

he follows the money and the gifts and the invitations to all the gentry parties."

"You're forgetting something, Neville."

"What's that?"

"He'll do you people favors. But he stops at murder. He's never covered for a murder."

"You sure about that?"

"Yeah, I am. Because I know him. He does you favors, but that would never include murder. And if I let you have at Tolan and Rooney on the trail, he'd see both of us hang. Now let's head for the jail."

Gomez sat at the front desk inside the marshal's office, spurred boots hanging off the desktop. He was examining with great concentration something that he had just picked from his nose as they were entering.

"I am not an educated man," Gomez said. "I am, in fact, a simple man. So I do not know why taking things from the nose is considered improper. People pick inside their nose and someone sees them — and the picker gets all embarrassed and ashamed. It is a natural and normal function. I do not understand the shame of it."

"You looked like a man who pondered the great questions of mankind, Gomez," Prine said. "And I was right."

Gomez had a vicious-looking dagger sitting on his kneecap. He leaned forward, plucked it from its position, and then used its tip to flick away the material he'd just picked from his nose.

"We want to see Valdez," Neville said. "Now."

Gomez slowly raised his eyes to meet Neville's.

"I can tell you're an important man, senor. You treat people the way important men treat people." He brought his feet down and sat forward in his chair. "With contempt." The blade of his dagger was pointed at Neville. "Like the shit that comes from the holes in animals. That is how you treat the likes of me."

Most of Gomez's words were said sardonically. As if he were putting on an act meant to put them off or vaguely frighten them. But his speech about Neville being an important man seemed truly angry. Prine's hand hovered near his Colt. He was half expecting Gomez to fling himself on Neville.

But when he spoke next, he was in control of himself and the tone was again sardonic. "If you will be so kind as to wait here, Mr. Important Man, I will see if the marshal can see you now."

He turned and walked back into the depths of the office.

"Drunken bastard," Neville said. "He's dangerous."

"Yes, especially if you happen to be an important man."

"What Gomez — and most people, for that matter — need to learn is that there are good and bad rich people the same as there are good and bad poor people."

"I guess I'd have to agree with that," Prine said, "but bad rich people tend to stand out a little more."

Gomez came halfway back down the hall. He waved them to join him and then led them to the office where they'd been before, to Valdez's office.

Valdez had taken off his jacket and now stood in a fancy white shirt with heavy black stitches along the seams. Blood was spattered everywhere on the shirt. Valdez's knuckles were torn and bloody. He obviously had spent some time interrogating Tolan and Rooney.

"God must be making men stronger these days," Valdez said, "or else I am getting weaker. In the old days, my hands would not have been cut up by the likes of those two confidence men."

"They're not just confidence men any

longer," Neville said. "They're murderers. They killed my sister."

"And so they did," Valdez said, once more affecting his pose of sorrow.

"They admitted it?" Prine said.

"Oh, yes. It took almost no persuasion at all and they admitted it. But they said it was an accident."

Prine said, "You don't cut somebody's throat by accident."

Valdez frowned. "Confidence men, murderers, and now bald-faced liars. They did not tell me that they'd cut her throat. I am most sorry, Senor Neville."

Neville said, "I want them turned over to us. Now. And no more bullshit."

Valdez looked hurt. He was a good actor. "Please, inasmuch as I represent the town of Picaro, please do not go around telling people that Marshal Valdez was anything less than cooperative. For that is all I care to be."

"You knew where those two were all along," Prine said. "If we hadn't found them ourselves, you wouldn't even have mentioned them."

Valdez took to clucking. "Now you accuse me, too? A fellow man of law and order?"

"We want them now," Prine said.

"And of course you shall have them."

"Now?" said Neville.

"Once you pay their bail."

"We don't have to bail them out." Prine said. "We're acting on behalf of Sheriff Daly."

"That is true, yes. But they must be bailed out first. That is how we do things here. Even lawmen must put up the bail if they want the prisoners released to their custody."

Prine had the feeling that Valdez made this up as he went along.

Neville said, "Your blood money. Prine told me all about you and this so-called judge."

"He is a man of utmost honor and integrity, this honorable jurist. Say what you want about Marshal Valdez. But leave your gringo tongue off the judge."

Prine said, "How much is the bail?"

"Ten thousand dollars," Valdez said.

"A fucking shakedown," Neville said. He'd told Prine that he'd brought plenty of money along in case bribes were in order. But bribes this big he hadn't counted on.

"Such language is not tolerated within these walls. I myself attend mass every day. As does the entire Valdez family."

Prine said, "We don't have much choice."

"It's a shakedown," Neville said.

"That's true. But we're not going to get them otherwise."

"He can do this?"

"He can inside the town limits of Picaro."

"Isn't that always the way with partners?" Valdez said, his voice showing he was pleased now. He knew he was going to get his money. "One man is reasonable." He nodded to Prine. "And the other is always *un*reasonable." He nodded to Neville.

Prine said, "You're offering a twenty-five-thousand-dollar reward. This'll save you a lot of money. Plus which, we don't have a lot of choice in the matter."

"And we get them now?"

"Right now," Valdez said. "Five minutes at the most."

"You're as much of a crook as they are," Neville said.

"I just thank God you did not accuse me of being a murderer," Valdez said. "Now, if you will give me your bank draft, I will help you bring justice to these men."

"You're a thief," Neville said.

"This is simply the way we do business in Picaro. I do not make the laws here. I merely follow them. Now, why don't you take seats while I get the men for you?"

Chapter Sixteen

Greenbacks. Thousand-dollar denominations. A fat fistful. Greenbacks flicking one after the other as Neville counted them in the absence of the good Marshal Valdez.

"Shakedown," Neville said.

"What a shock. Valdez shaking people down."

"I thought crooked lawmen were pretty much out of the picture these days."

"I'd say Valdez here is an exception."

"Why the hell don't you do something?"

"Look, Neville. I know he's a pig and you know he's a pig. But the thing is to get the two men. We can worry about Valdez later."

Neville sighed. "I guess you're right. I'm doing this for Cassie."

Prine nodded. "That's the thing to remember."

Heavy footsteps in the hall outside Valdez's office made both Prine and Neville look up. And then they were there, preceding Valdez into the office.

Tolan and Rooney. You could see faint bruises on their faces from Valdez's interrogation. No look of remorse or fear in their eyes. Dirty, their clothes stained and soiled, their handcuffs heavy and cinched tight, they could have stood in for dozens and dozens of men Prine had arrested in his time.

"Gentlemen, I give you the men you have been searching for for such a long time," Valdez said grandly.

"About twenty-four hours, actually," Prine said.

"The men you intend to bring to justice," Valdez said. "The men who sinned so gravely against your sister, Mr. Neville."

"Does this asshole ever shut up?" Rooney said. Even in a suit that now resembled dirty rags, there was still the air of a sharper about him. The almost pretty face, the cunning eyes, the air of shabby sophistication.

Valdez slapped him hard across the mouth. Blood stained the end of Rooney's lips. "A man who goes to mass every day does not want to hear language like this. I have told you that many times, Mr. Rooney."

Valdez turned to Neville. "Here is my end of the bargain. I assume you have yours ready for me."

215

Neville laid ten thousand dollars on the desk. Once this was done, and without warning, he walked over to Tolan and smashed him in the nose. Crack of blood; spray of blood. But he wasn't done. He struck Tolan so hard in the sternum that Tolan shot backward, tripping over a chair and falling in an ungainly pile on the floor.

"Hey, Mex," Rooney said to Valdez. "You can't let them do this to us."

But it was too late to stop Neville. He used the toe of his Texas boot on Rooney, and judging from the screams, he used it effectively. Rooney tried to clutch his crotch, but the handcuffs made it difficult. He went to the floor in three folds, the last one giving him the freedom to slam his forehead hard against the floor. He was out.

Neville was about to kick him in the head, but Prine yanked on his arm.

"You've had your fun for the day," Prine said. "They're under my jurisdiction now and we're taking them back in one piece."

Neville was not happy.

"She wasn't your sister, Prine."

Prine decided not to tell Neville what his sister really thought of him.

They rode till late in the afternoon, covering about half the trek back home.

216

Valdez had horses saddled and ready for the prisoners.

Prine and Neville rode in the back. Tolan and Rooney said little. A few times they talked with each other. Prine told them to shut up.

Neville was sullen. He was now more like the man Prine had met at recital the other night. When he did speak, there was an impudence to his tone that Prine resented. Neville was apparently under the impression that Prine worked for him.

"I have to piss," Rooney said over his shoulder.

"We'll make camp pretty soon," Prine said.

"I can't hold it."

"Then wet yourself, you bastard," Neville said. His hand flew to his gun, but Prine was ahead of him. His Colt was aimed directly at Neville.

"I thought we had an agreement, Neville."

"Not that I know of."

"Put that hand back on the saddle horn."

"I can't take being around these two. All I see is Cassie."

"Then maybe you should ride on ahead a ways so you don't have to see them."

Neville sulked, said nothing.

"You hear what I said, Neville?"

"I heard."

"Then do we have an agreement? We get these prisoners back to Sheriff Daly the same condition they're in now."

Neville wouldn't give him the satisfaction of a verbal agreement. He just nodded his head.

They rode on.

The last two hours of the day's ride went slowly. Prine was eager to be back in Claybank. The curiously silent prisoners were risky enough, even when they were handcuffed, but Neville was the most dangerous of all. His rage over the fate of his sister, however understandable, kept Prine tensed up.

They would occasionally come upon a farm that looked perfect — always from a distance, of course, denying Prine the view of what the hardscrabble places looked like close up — the sort of place he sometimes daydreamed about owning. A pastoral life. Wife, kids, eating off the land.

But the grousing of the prisoners in front of him brought him back from his flights of idealized life. Neither Tolan nor Rooney appeared to be comfortable on horseback.

Tolan complained about the horse wandering, the horse slowing, the horse speeding up — all defying Tolan's wishes.

Rooney was simply afraid of his animal. A couple of times, when the horse started to buck a little, Rooney let go with a childlike cry. *Daddy, please come take me down from this terrible beast.*

What a trio they were.

At any moment, Neville could decide the hell with it and open fire on the prisoners. Backshoot them. Kill them. It certainly wasn't impossible. Prine wanted to salvage this whole shameful episode by making it as right as he could. He wanted to bring his prisoners in alive and legal. And then he wanted to tell Sheriff Daly everything. Prine was responsible for Cassie's murder. The guilt would always be with him. But maybe by bringing in Tolan and Rooney, and telling the truth, he could start to make amends for the stupid, selfish plan for riches and power that had resulted in a young woman's death.

When they finally made camp within a small stand of elm trees, everybody got to stretch, piss, and give their saddle sores a rest. Tolan walked up a slight grassy incline. No reason a man couldn't run with handcuffs on. Men had done it plenty of

219

times before. Prine decided to do a little law enforcement. He fired a single shot that chewed up dust right next to Tolan's wandering feet. Tolan, surprised and scared, jumped a quarter foot, then turned around and spat in Prine's direction.

"Next time you go sight-seeing," Prine told him, "you check with me first."

"Someday I'll have the gun," Tolan said. "We'll see how you like it then."

Prine took care of the horses. Got them watered and fed and bedded down for the night. He liked the horses far better than the men he was with.

Neville built a fire. It was a good one. Prine was surprised that Neville was good at the outdoors. He figured Neville would have all such things done by one of his manservants. He was probably being too hard on Neville. A man's sister murdered like that, he'd have one hell of a time keeping his hands off the killers.

Rooney was saying, "You won't believe this, Deputy, but my father is a very important lawyer back in Cincinnati."

"Good for him."

Rooney laughed. "They tell everybody I'm dead. I'm told my dear mother fainted dead away when my brother told her that the reason they hadn't been able to find me was that I was in prison."

"How many times I got to hear this stupid story?" Tolan said.

"Now, Tolan here," Rooney said, sounding awful pleased with himself for a man in handcuffs, "Tolan here was born under a rock. No known parents. When he wants lawmen to feel sorry for him, he always trots out all his stories about his little sister. He wants you to feel sorry for him. But he just makes himself more pathetic than he already is." Prine wasn't paying a hell of a lot of attention. He was hungry and waiting for food.

The grub they'd brought consisted of jerky and rolls. Neville had also brought some coffee and a tin pot. Prine was about the only one who could stand it. He'd been prepared for it by drinking Daly's coffee.

"I want you boys to move a little closer to the fire tonight," Prine said.

"Worried we might get cold, Deputy?" Rooney said. "That's right nice of you."

"I want you in range so I don't have any trouble seeing you."

"Gosh, and here I thought you were just worried about us getting cold."

Prine walked over to his saddle and plucked out his Winchester. He came back to Tolan and Rooney and said, "Stick your feet out."

"Why the hell should I?" Tolan said.

"Because I'm going to start breaking your toes one by one if you don't."

He took their boots off. Threw them in weeds a few yards from the campsite. Into the darkness.

"What the hell you do that for?" Tolan said.

"In case we try to make a break," Rooney said. "It'll take us some time to find our boots."

Tolan grinned. "I knew you was afraid of us, Deputy. You're tryin' to stack the whole deck in your favor tonight, right?"

"Sure, I'm afraid of you, Tolan. I'm not used to being around men who'd do to a woman what you did to poor Cassie. I'll do anything I need to to make sure you're still here in the morning."

Tolan grinned again. "I knew you was scared. You always try to act so cool. But you're scared. You know what we'll do to you if you give us half a chance."

Rooney said, "Sometimes, Tolan here likes to hear himself talk. I'm afraid I'm guilty of that myself. Sometimes."

"Go to sleep," Prine said.

"God, those feet of yours stink, Tolan,"

Rooney said. "I can smell them way over here."

"Don't start on me, Rooney. I could still smash your face in even with these cuffs on."

"Both of you shut up," Prine said.

He went over and poured more coffee into the tin cup. He sat staring into the fire, thinking of so many things and yet nothing at all.

"Who gets first watch?" Neville said as the clouds sprawled golden and gray and wine-colored behind the snowy mountain peaks.

"I do," Prine said. "I also get the second."

"What the hell're you talking about?"

"What I'm talking about is no way am I leaving you alone with those two."

"You don't want to make an enemy of me, Prine. You've got to live in Claybank when this is all over."

"So do you," Prine said. "I'm sorry about your sister, and I'd just as soon return the favor and cut those two up same as they cut Cassie up. But I take my job serious, Neville. I'm bringing them in alive. So you might as well take advantage of it and get yourself some sleep."

Prine went over and checked the prisoners out.

They still didn't talk much, not even to each other. They just watched him as he checked their handcuffs.

"You don't let him at us," Rooney said.

"That sonofabitch is crazy," Tolan said.

"Yeah?" Prine said. "Well, if he is crazy, I wonder who made him that way? Most regular gents do go a little crazy when two pieces of shit like you murder their sister."

"I want to see Daly," Rooney said.

"He won't go any easier on you," Prine said. "And he'll probably even hang you two personally. He liked Cassie. Everybody did. Now, shut up and go to sleep. We'll be rollin' out of here just after five."

Neville made his peace with his bedroll and the ground, which was still damp from last night's rain.

Prine sat nearby on a rock. He kept the fire going. He also kept swigging coffee. Staying up all night was never easy.

"Thanks for that, Prine."

"For what?"

"For calling them pieces of shit like that. I was afraid you were forgetting about Cassie."

"All I was doing was remembering that I have to bring them in alive unless they do something."

"Well, thanks. I appreciate it anyway."

Full night came, inking the sky, darkening the shapes of trees and foothills and the land itself. After a time, the world around him seemed unreal. Only the fire and the three men lying around it existed. The rest of the world was darkness, full of life noises and sometimes death noises, those odd quick struggles of night creatures.

The fire wasn't up to keeping him warm. Most of the wood had been burned up. He kept telling himself he needed to get up and find some more wood. But he couldn't escape his thoughts, a sort of reverie. He needed to talk to Daly and set it all straight. If there was prison time ahead, so be it. Then he wanted to talk to Lucy and see if she'd take him back.

He had just started to lean in for some more coffee when the rock hit him. There was just time enough to see the impossible — Tolan on his feet, one handcuff dangling free from his wrist, a fist-sized rock in his hand. And then the rock being thrown with great speed and efficiency right at him.

Pain registered, and then a confusion of pain, momentary blindness, and a desperate attempt to find his Colt and fire.

Nothingness was the last to come. Cold

shooting through his body. Shivering, teeth-chattering cold, a damned good approximation of death. And then a distant sense of himself toppling over, hitting the ground hard enough to jar his teeth.

And then —

Nightbirds. Their cries. Wind. Its creeping coldness. Constriction. Steel on his wrists.

Prine forced his eyes open.

He lay on his side. The fire was out, ash.

Despite the enormous headache that kept pressing him down, he managed to sit up high enough to see Neville's body on the other side of the dead fire. Neville lay flat on his face. Prine couldn't get much detail from here. Was Neville even alive? Was he handcuffed?

Tolan and Rooney. Where the hell were they? What the hell had happened?

The rock. The pain. The blackness.

How Tolan had managed to slip out of his handcuffs was a question for another time. Now the important thing was to go after them.

After he gained his wobbly legs, he found out just how difficult finding them would be. They'd either swatted away Prine and Neville's horses or they'd taken them with them. The horses were gone.

He stumbled across the edge of the ash that had been the fire and dropped to his haunches next to Neville.

"Neville. Wake up, Neville."

Neville had also been handcuffed. A wound showed itself on the side of his forehead. A rock had no doubt hit him, too.

Neville didn't respond. Prine leaned closer, listened for Neville's breathing.

Faint. Ragged. But steady. That was one good sign, anyway.

Prine staggered to his feet and went in search of the coffeepot. He needed some, and so did Neville. He'd drink it cold if he had to.

He staggered toward the coffeepot, scrounged around for the tin cup, found it, and then stumbled back to Neville.

"Neville, Neville, wake up."

He shook him a little with his cuffed hands. He had to be careful. Neville might have some kind of concussion.

Eventually, Neville turned a mud-streaked profile to Prine. The damned ground really was muddy.

"What happened?"

"They had a key."

Neville's rage shed some of his fuzziness.

Holding his head miserably, he sat up and said, "That sonofabitch Valdez sold it to him."

"Probably."

"When this is all over, that's the bastard I'm going after. Valdez."

"We're sitting out here in the middle of nowhere, Neville. Your threats sound sort of pathetic since we don't have guns or horses."

"They took our horses?"

"Afraid so."

"What the hell're we going to do?" Neville asked.

"We're not that far away from the Lattimore spread. About a morning's walk."

"That's a hell of a long walk."

Prine shrugged. "You think of a better way of getting there?"

Chapter Seventeen

Prine had either underestimated the length of the walk or overestimated their strength. They moved sluggishly through grazing land, their time not even improving that much when they reached the stage road. They'd had a hard thirty-six hours and it had cost them energy and resolve.

"The only thing that's keeping me going," Neville said several times, "is knowing that they're going to hang soon."

All Prine did was nod. If hatred was the fuel that kept Neville going, so be it. Prine had his own fuel. He wanted to admit what he'd done and try to put his life back together.

At midpoint in their trek, Prine saw a wagon in the distance. He put all his strength into chasing after it, shouting, waving his arms. For nothing. He never came close to reaching it.

For his part, Neville took to standing on large boulders and gazing off into the distance. He looked like a fake Indian in a Wild West show, his hand covering his brow so he could see better, his posture rigid as a pointer's when it spots its prey. It looked dramatic as hell but didn't get them anywhere.

They reached the Lattimore ranch around three in the afternoon. Dave Lattimore was just coming out of the barn, a small, quick man in a flannel shirt and Levi's, wiping his forehead with his sleeve. When he saw the two men, he started looking around for their horses.

"Afternoon," he said.

"Afternoon," Prine said.

"Lattimore, we need some horses and a couple of rifles. I'll pay you double what they're worth."

The old, familiar Neville was putting in an appearance again, and Prine wasn't happy about it.

He gave Lattimore a quick version of everything that had happened.

"You think they're still around here?" Lattimore said.

"They are if they're headed to Denver," Prine said. "They'll be settlin' in for the night pretty soon. If we go all night, we might be able to find them."

"No offense, Prine, but neither of you fellas look like you could *last* all night."

"We didn't ask for any of your Farmer

230

Bob wisdom, Lattimore," Neville snapped. "We asked for horses and rifles. Now, can you set us up?"

Lattimore didn't like being talked to this way, obviously. But in order to help Prine, he nodded and said, "Yeah, I can set you up."

"I appreciate this, Dave," Prine said as they headed for a small rope corral set off from the outbuildings. The shadows were long, heavy, now that the sun was beginning its descent. Lattimore's wife was getting supper ready. You could smell it on the air. Prine had thoughts of a home-cooked meal, a leisurely one, topped off with a good cigar and some good sipping whiskey.

While Prine and Neville looked over the horses, Lattimore went up to the house for the guns.

"Dave's a good man," Prine said.

"I'm sure he is."

"I'd appreciate it if you'd treat him that way."

"What? I wasn't treating him that way?"

For the first time, Prine realized that Neville here probably wasn't even aware of acting like a shit sometimes. His behavior was probably so ingrained — hell, he'd grown up rich and powerful, why wouldn't he just naturally assume that most people were put on earth to play subjects to his role as conqueror? — he didn't even hear himself. Or see the resentment in the eyes of the people he insulted.

"Just don't treat him like one of your servants," Prine said. "He's not, and I'm not, either."

"Well, hell, man, I didn't mean to insult him."

"Maybe not," Prine said. "But you did a damned good job of it anyway."

Prine took a dun, Neville a pinto. They walked them up to the barn, where they found a couple of old saddles.

Neville looked unhappy about having to set his royal ass on a saddle this worn, but at least he had the good sense not to say anything about it.

Lattimore appeared a few minutes later. He handed Prine a Winchester and Neville a Sharps that had been old ten years before.

"Best I could do," he said to Neville.

Prine fought a smile. He was sure that Lattimore had dug up the oldest weapon he could find for Neville. If Neville knew this, he didn't let on. He was behaving well since Prine had ragged on him about treating Lattimore better. He was like a dog brought to heel.

They were just ready to saddle up when Betty Lattimore, pretty and plump in blue gingham and a white apron, hurried down to them.

"Figured you boys'd be hungry," she said.

They took their food over to a small table in the backyard. Slices of beef and a boiled potato and peas, probably from her garden on the far side of the house. They ate with the innocence and fury of predatory animals. "And you're invited to sleep here overnight if you'd like."

"Thank you very much, Mrs. Lattimore," Neville said in a voice so formal and polite that Prine actually quit shoveling food into his mouth for a few seconds. "You and your husband have already done plenty, and I plan to pay you back as soon as this is all done with."

"Why, we're practically neighbors, Mr. Neville. So there's no call to talk about paying us back. I'm sure you'd do the same thing for us."

Neville looked confused briefly. Somebody was turning down his offer to pay them back? He was used to paying people off. Money was the currency, not friendship. That was startling enough. But then, she'd said that he would do the same thing

233

for her. But would he? Prine could see this thought process. It would be too much to say that Neville was having any kind of conversion to the goodwill of the common man here, but clearly he was forming a favorable impression of these people.

"Yes," Neville said, "I guess I would do the same thing for you."

He glanced at Prine as he said this. Prine gave him a doubtful look.

They left just as dusk was streaking the sky with its richest colors, the colors that only Eastern potentates were said to possess, colors that were the secret treasures handed down from ancient Egypt, colors, or so it was claimed, that no other civilization could duplicate — mauve and purple gold and green the color of a cat's eye.

Both men huddled inside their ponchos. They knew that soon enough the land would shimmer and shine with frost. Ice might even cover the creeks and the river by the time of the midnight moon.

Distant drums, having nothing to do with them, came from Ute camps scattered around the hills to the west.

Neither man said much. There wasn't much to say. Once in a while they'd piss and moan about how their asses hurt from

their saddles, how the dropping temperature was beginning to test the strength of
their ponchos, how when it was all over a
bed would feel very good.

Neville, of course, had small moments of
rage. Obviously, the man couldn't help
himself. He'd start thinking of his sister
and he'd go wild for a few minutes.

Their first stop came around nine
o'clock when they saw the remnants of a
mining town. An entire block of businesses
were boarded up. Maybe two dozen tiny
houses stood dark. Somebody had shot out
all the stained-glass windows in the
church.

The whipping and whining wind didn't
exactly help Prine's sense of desolation.
My God, not only had the gold boom gone
bust in this place, he wondered if a plague
hadn't visited it. He thought of images he'd
learned about in school, how in medieval
days the bubonic plague would literally
wipe out the entire populations of some
small towns.

They tied their horses to a hitching post
in front of the saloon. The batwing doors,
silhouetted against dim, flickering lamplight from inside, hung on one hinge each. A
player piano badly out of sync and tune
rolled through "Camptown Lady," somehow

making it sound like a dirge.

Prine was so tired that all sorts of silly childhood images came to him. Ghosts, inside; or ghouls, the living dead a la Edgar Allan Poe. Or maybe spirits so hideous there weren't even any names for them.

They took their rifles with them.

The way the wind was whipping, one of the batwings tore free and fell to the floor. Prine pushed on inside.

The sight before him resembled a stage set that had been deserted long enough to be shrouded with thick, dusty cobwebs. A long pine bar was on the right wall, a long dusty mirror running parallel to it. Empty tables and chairs filled up most of the space except for a small stage against which the player piano was pushed. Rats were everywhere, paying no attention whatsoever to the intruders. There must have been a dozen good-sized rats on top of the piano, scurrying about in frenzy. Needing, wanting — but not finding — food.

Only after a time did they cast their tiny red eyes on the newcomers. You could almost hear them begin to calculate what these strange upright creatures would taste like.

Neville shot three of them. The explosion of his Sharps was almost loud enough to tear the wide chandelier above them from its mooring.

"Happy now?" Prine said.

"I don't have the right to shoot rats?"

"You don't have the right to waste ammunition, is what you don't have."

In the mere, drab light, Neville's face filled with blood.

"I guess that was pretty stupid."

"You won't get any argument from me," Prine said.

Prine began to walk around the saloon. He wondered how long it had been since this place had heard and seen human revelry. The rats might dance on some spectral midnight. But it had been a long time since saloon gals had prodded old sourdoughs to drink some more of the watered-down liquor, and high-kicking dancers had exposed their frill-covered bottoms to the delight of the all-male audience.

Prine heard it first. He thought it was just one more variation on the eerie tones the winds made. But after it sounded two or three times, he recognized the gasping noise, like that of a man who couldn't catch his breath. A drowning man, perhaps.

Neville had climbed the stairs and was

inspecting the second floor. Prine stayed on the ground floor, trying to find the source of the strange sound. He finally located it behind the bar, the one place he hadn't thought to look.

The old man lay on his back. From the dark circle on his filthy gray shirt, Prine assumed the man had been shot in the chest. He'd been hit in such a way that he couldn't breathe well. When he tried to speak or call out in simple syllables, the words would stop somewhere in his throat and he would clutch his throat with both hands, as if his throat had been cut.

Prine grabbed the only source of light, the ancient lantern on top of the bar, and held it down to the man. The wound, as he'd guessed, was in the chest, though further away from the heart than he'd suspected. There was a wooden box on top of the back bar. Inside, Prine found two canteens. They were both full. He untied his bandanna and soaked it with water.

He spent the next ten minutes exhausting the full extent of his medical knowledge — pulse points, eye dilation, breathing, consciousness. None was very good. The old man muttered words from time to time but nothing Prine could understand.

Neville showed up and watched as Prine cleaned up the old man's wound so he could get a better look at it.

"They figured he was dead," Neville said.

"They weren't far wrong."

"He going to make it?"

"Take a miracle."

"Didn't find anything upstairs. But this must've been a nice little place at one time."

Maybe because they were talking, maybe because the old man knew how close he was to dying and he wanted to talk to somebody — whatever, he sat up a little and fully opened his eyes.

"You ain't them, is you?" he said. His teeth were blackened stubs. His mouth was circle of scabs. He had to blink his eyes to focus. "No, I can see you now. You ain't them."

"They shot you?"

Phlegm clogged his chest and throat.

"They didn't see nobody in here except ole Midnight, so they just figured they had the place to themselves. They wanted to sleep before nightfall." He started coughing up blood. Prine held his frail upper body until the coughing stopped. "When they found me — I always sleep in the back room — they figured I might tell the law on them. Stupid bastards. Closest town is Claybank, and an old man like me ain't never goin' to Claybank and live to tell about it. The one named Tolan, he's the bastard that shot me." Then: "Midnight! Midnight!"

Prine wondered if the old man was hallucinating. There was no evidence of anybody else in the place. Maybe the old man was recalling a childhood friend.

But the old man grew more and more agitated, cried louder and louder for this "Midnight!"

And damned if Midnight didn't put in an appearance. A raven of vast proportion and eerie gaze, it didn't simply fly through the air, it smashed its way, the flutter of its wing violent as a terrible storm. It landed on the bar above the old man. Perched there, looked down at him.

"I just wanted to see him again before I passed." Then: "You been a good friend, Midnight."

The sleek, shiny, somehow supernatural bird made a sound in its own throat. A deep rumbling kind of music that was sustained for several seconds. A music dark as its feathers.

The old man said, "They said they was

gonna try and make a train tomorrow morning. Junction Gap. You get 'em for me, will ya? Now Midnight's gonna be all alone."

They buried him out back.

Midnight seemed to understand what was going on.

In the moonlight, he sat sentrylike, upon the fresh earth that Prine and Neville had turned over. The raven raised its regal head once to look at the moon. The dark music sounded again in chest and throat. But this time it expelled the sound, letting it echo off the ragged rock hills and work its trembling, oddly frightening way through the night. Other animals responded in the far-flung darkness and made their own sounds. Even the horses Lattimore had loaned them joined in.

Prine said some prayers for the old man, the prayers of his childhood. He didn't say them often, so many of the words were wrong. He wasn't even sure there was a God, at least not a God as Sunday school teachers espoused anyway. But he did believe in some kind of universal spirit that was the cement of not only this planet but the entire cosmos. He was appealing to that spirit now to take the old man to a good and true place.

Ten minutes after burying the old man, they were on their way again. Now they knew where Tolan and Rooney were headed. They planned to meet the two at the Junction Gap train depot.

Chapter Eighteen

Karl Tolan had never forgotten how his three-year-old sister Daisy died. He still had nightmares about it. He was seven at the time.

He'd been playing behind the crude slab cabin his father had built when he heard a cry unlike any he'd ever heard Daisy make before.

She was off playing on the edge of their property. She liked to pick "pretty flowers," as she often tried to say. What she picked was dandelions.

Karl's mother was inside making bread, his father off trapping.

The cry.

His body wanted to do two things at once — freeze in place and run. He was afraid to find out what had happened to his sister.

He forced himself to go to her.

Her tiny hands were raised almost in prayer to the sky, blood running from them as blood ran in gouts from her mouth.

He knelt next to her, the cry scaring him

as nothing ever had, screaming "What's wrong, Daisy? What's wrong, Daisy!" until his mother pushed him out of the way and put her fingers in Daisy's mouth. Daisy cried louder and louder; not even her mother's fingers could halt the plea.

His mother pulled pieces of glass from Daisy's mouth. Karl had a hard time recognizing what they were at first, they were so bloody. But then he recognized where they had come from. He'd broken a bottle yesterday while he was playing games by himself. He swore to pick up the glass when he was finished playing. Otherwise his father would take a strap to him.

But he'd forgotten somehow. And now Daisy, who had apparently mistaken the broken glass for pieces of candy, had started stuffing the glass into her mouth, not only cutting herself but swallowing some of the tinier pieces.

Daisy lived less than ten hours. The way his folks glared at him, he didn't have to ask if they blamed him. Of course they did.

They buried her on a hill where the winds were like cool magic in the spring months and where the surrounding trees took fire in the autumn.

Less than a day after they buried her, some coyotes dug her up and ate most of her. His father killed them, but by then it was too late.

His mother never recovered. Two years later, she smashed a bottle one night when his father was on one of his trapping trips. Karl was so sound a sleeper, he didn't hear the breaking bottle or the rest of it. She hadn't screamed, made a fuss. Which had been very much like her.

She hadn't wanted to take any chances. She slashed both her throat and her wrists. By morning, when he woke up and found her on the far side of the cabin in her bed, her skin was blue-gray in color. He had never seen her eyes so sad. Not scared. Just plain old sad. He'd done it, he knew. When he'd helped kill his little sister, he'd helped kill his mother, too.

After his father got back and they buried her, he got out his long piece of leather and went to work on Karl. He drew blood. He slashed his buttocks to the point where Karl's legs were numb, not just his buttocks. Finally, Karl fell to the floor, sobbing, pleading for his father to stop.

A few minutes later, he heard the father outside. There was just the one shot. Karl knew immediately what it was. He'd have a lot of work to do, burying the two of them. He wanted good, deep graves.

He worked a full day and a half on those graves and he was proud of them. He shot and killed six coyotes in the process. For headstones he took large round rocks that sparkled like fool's gold and drew their names in heavy pencil.

He knew the coyotes would get them, but by then he'd be gone — and damned if he wasn't. Just going on eleven, he packed everything he owned and jammed it all into his father's carpetbag and then headed off to Dexter, the small town to the north. He'd already pretty much forgotten about his folks. They'd never especially liked him and he'd never especially liked them.

Who he couldn't forget was Daisy. Poor little Daisy.

Big for his age, and already with a frightening temper — it not only frightened other people, it also frightened him — he set off west.

Three weeks shy of his fifteenth birthday, he met Rooney in a most unusual way. He was standing on a street corner in Denver and happened to see Rooney, a red-haired runt, snatch a bag of groceries from an old woman. Rooney took off with the groceries. A cop just happened along. One of those coincidences that happen in real life but that you could never get away with in books or on the stage. The cop started chasing him and was closing on him.

Until Karl offered his services by innocently stepping into the cop's path and nearly knocking the man down. The thief got away. What Karl got was screamed at by the bully-faced copper.

Three blocks away, Rooney fell into step with him and said, "You could come in handy, kid."

The "kid" thing amused Karl. Rooney looked several years younger than he did.

From then on, the two became friends of a sort, even though Karl didn't especially like Rooney or trust him or have any respect for him. Friends — even though Rooney thought Karl was stupid, sneaky, and too often reluctant to do what Rooney told him to — friends of a sort.

All these years later, in a saloon in Junction Gap, waiting for a train that was still several hours away, talking to the man he didn't like, trust, or have any respect for, Karl Tolan said, "You think they figured out we paid off Valdez to give us the key?"

"Not all men are stupid, Karl."

"Meaning what?"

"Meaning that not all men are stupid."

"Meaning me."

"Uh-oh, Karl's having his monthly visitor again."

"I hate when you say that."

"Yeah, well, there are a few things I don't like to hear *you* say, either."

"Yeah? Like what?"

"I don't want to argue, Karl."

"Just gimme one example."

Rooney sighed. "You'll just get pissed the way you always do when I offer constructive criticism."

"C'mon, just one example."

"You never fucking take a bath."

"Oh, yeah? I took a bath last week."

"That's just my point, Karl. You need to take a bath more often than once a week."

"What, so I can look like some dude the way you do?"

"See what I mean? I offer you constructive criticism — and at your request, mind you — and you go and get pissy on me."

"Nobody's getting pissy."

Rooney smiled. Pure ice. "Yeah, I noticed that."

"Maybe I won't be goin' to St. Louis with you, after all."

"Fine. It's a free country."

"Maybe I'll go to California."

"Whatever you want to do, Karl. It's up to you."

"Yeah," Karl said, sounding almost mystical, "California."

Rooney just couldn't seem to resist.

"Is this," he said, "anything like the time you were going to go to Montana or anything like the time you were going to go to Alabama or anything like the time you were going to go to Mexico?"

"You really don't think I can pull away from you, do you?"

Rooney gave him his most superior smile. "I was just asking, Karl. Just asking."

With seven hours to go before train time, Rooney told Karl he was tired and would get some sleep back in his hotel room. Emphasis on *his*. Usually, the two men shared a room, not exactly being in the robber baron category.

This time was different. And for a good reason.

Before heading back to the hotel, Rooney stopped off at a shop, bought himself a couple of good stogies and some magazines to read on the train during the daylight hours.

He also used this time to plan on how he was going to break into Karl's room.

For his part, Tolan went to a whore-

249

house. He paid six dollars for a lady with an ass of considerable size and a mouth as nasty as a cowhand's.

"You make good money on a gent like me," Tolan told her. "I'm quick."

When she saw how quick, she said, "You sure weren't kiddin' about bein' quick. You're about the quickest man I ever seed, in fact."

As he walked to the hotel, Tolan kept chewing on her remark. Quick, huh? He didn't mind himself sayin' he was quick in a joshin' sort of way. But the way *she* said it, he wondered if she really *was* joshin'.

Thinking about it soured him.

And then all of Rooney's superior bullshit came back to him too. Not takin' a bath often enough. Just because Tolan wasn't a dandy like Rooney. Just because Tolan found taking a bath to be a really complicated task. You had to take your clothes off, you had to lower yourself into the tub, you had to soak and scrub and get soap in your eyes and fart in the water, and then you had to get up and dry yourself off and put your clothes back on — it was an additional burden if you had to take your clothes to some Chinese laundry in advance — and then you had to put your socks and your boots back on. Who the hell wanted to spend all that time doin' all that bullshit?

Besides, splash on a little bit of that smelly stuff he bought off that barber in Idaho that time, who could tell you *hadn't* taken a bath?

What he should do now was get on a horse and ride as wide of that sawed-off little prick Rooney as he could.

That's what he should do.

But much as he hated to acknowledge that Rooney was right, he'd tried it so many times before. Got right up to the point of leaving — told Rooney off right to his face — and then just couldn't quite do it. Couldn't quite get on the horse. Couldn't quite leave.

But this time, dammit —

And then he got one hell of a good idea.

Rooney knew that this was not without risk. If Tolan caught him, he just might think of all the ways Rooney had pushed him around, humiliated him, stolen from him, and generally been what you might call a real bad friend.

So.

So he had to be very, very careful.

He had to get Tolan's money and then clear the hell out. He had a horse waiting

251

for him at the livery. He hoped that he would be a good ten miles away before Tolan ever figured out what had happened.

Getting into the room was no problem. He'd merely slipped the desk clerk some extra money.

That was the easy part — the only easy part.

Tolan could turn any room he squatted in into something that even barnyard animals would shun. There was Tolan's stench, for one thing. Rooney opened the window. There was Tolan's messiness, for another. You wouldn't think a carpetbag could hold such a cornucopia of junk — reeking clothes; a collection of photographs depicting bovine naked ladies; an array of patent medicines that offered to cure every disease known to men of all colors, creeds, and political persuasions; and fruit that was now covered with maggots. Tolan had been told by some barfly somewhere that fresh fruit was one good way of holding scurvy at bay. The trouble was (a) you couldn't always find fresh fruit and (b) fresh fruit didn't stay fresh very long and (c) Tolan hated fresh fruit. He claimed he always got pieces of it stuck in his teeth and spent half the night lying in his bed with a quiver of toothpicks trying to get rid of the aggravating little chunks between his rotted black teeth.

Not that a, b, or c made any difference to Tolan. Anytime they were anywhere near fresh fruit, Tolan would buy some and toss it into his carpetbag. And leave it there to rot. Who the hell wanted to lie awake half the night picking pieces of apples or plums or pears from your teeth?

Such was life with Tolan lo these many, many years.

Rooney searched for nearly fifteen minutes, stopping every time he heard footsteps coming up the stairs. Once he got nervous enough to excrete a sheath of cold sweat that covered his entire body. Another time his bowels clenched with such force that he doubled over. Damn.

None of the warnings turned into anything.

He went back to work. Under the bed. Under the mattress. The bureau drawers. The closet. The closet shelf. Nothing nothing nothing.

And then the most dreaded place of all: the inside of the carpetbag. Easy to imagine pit vipers in the deep, dark interior. Or hellfire-breathing dragons from the medieval fantasies of his boyhood reading. Maybe it was the portal to Hades itself and would suck him in with the force of a vortex.

Whatever it was, he knew it would be vile. God, just touching the outside of it was slimy enough. Imagine the inside.

He closed his eyes, held his breath, and began to insert his arm when —

He heard noise in the next room. *His* room.

His first thought was that Prine and Neville had found them. But how, with the head start they'd had? And how, when they had no idea where he and Tolan had been headed? He thought of the old man in the ghost town saloon. But how could the old man talk? Rooney had killed him personally. He'd checked his pulse at neck and wrist. Dead for sure.

Then who the hell was in there?

He realized what was going on soon enough. A hotel. Daytime. This was the busiest time of day for hotel thieves. They'd figure that most gents who stayed in a place like this would be drummers or traveling businessmen of some kind. The perfect time to toss a room and steal any and all of its valuables.

Frustrated that he hadn't found any of Tolan's money, he decided to have some fun. He'd kill the bastard who was in his room, was what he'd do. Then he'd wait for Tolan to show up and rob him right at gunpoint.

I want your money, Tolan. Or I'll kill you right here on the spot. And when he got the money, off he'd go. Points unknown. Tolan would never find him again, because Tolan would be dead.

For the first time in decades, Rooney would be a free man. No more dragging Tolan along. Being embarrassed by him whenever they were in polite company. Always worried that he'd get some dumb-ass idea to steal the money that Rooney had had the initiative to go out and steal himself.

Drawing his Colt, he crept out of Tolan's room, tiptoed to the adjoining room, and then flung the door open.

And it opened, all right — just fine and dandy, it opened. But the sight it opened on was enough to make Rooney slump against the door frame.

"What the hell're you doing in my room?" he said.

"You're s'posed to be the smart one, you figure it out." Tolan's Peacemaker was pointed right directly exactly unerringly at Rooney's head.

"You mean while I . . ."

Tolan smiled that dark rotted smile of his. "While you were robbin' my room, I was robbin' your room." The smile vanished. "Get in here and close the door."

"Thanks for inviting me into my own room."

"You're more than welcome."

Rooney closed the door and went over and sat down. The bed squeaked. A bird had left a streak of white shit on the window in Rooney's absence. Now he had Tolan to contend with.

"Guess what I found?" Tolan said, and held up an envelope that Rooney recognized right away.

"You bastard."

"For a smart man, you can be pretty dumb sometimes. Slitting a hole in the side of the mattress and shoving the envelope in there. All them little strings hanging out when you cut it open — hell, they led me right to the money, Rooney." The grubby smile again. "You, on the other hand, you didn't find nothin', did you?"

"You sonofabitch, Tolan."

Tolan stood up, confidently opened Rooney's envelope, peeked inside.

"I'm gonna have me one hell of a time in California, Rooney."

"Give me my money."

"Why the hell should I?"

"Because it's mine."

The smile. "You were tryin' to do the same thing to me. If you'da found it, you'da kept it."

"Tolan, listen, this is the most money —"

"You don't have to tell *me*, Rooney. This is the most money we ever had at one time. Least, that I know of, anyways. You pro'ly stole this much from me over the years, but I didn't know anything about it."

He crossed the room in three steps and slashed the barrel of his gun down across Rooney's jaw. A fireline of blood opened up instantly.

He stepped away. He knew that if he hit Rooney again, he wouldn't be able to stop hitting him. Too much anger stored up for too long. Too much humiliation. He'd heard Rooney making jokes about him to other people. Tolan knew how the sight of him disgusted people. Ever since little Daisy ate that glass, he'd been ugly. As if the same ugliness on his soul was now on his face. Both to his face and behind his back, Rooney had commented on this many, many times. Too many times for Tolan to handle any more.

"How was you gonna do it, Rooney, if you didn't find it in my room? Wait till it was dark and then backshoot me right before the train rolled in? You'd be in Denver by the time they figured out who killed me. Then it would all be yours."

"Why the hell'd you hit me?"

"Because I'm sick of your bullshit. Sick of the way you look down on me. You think I don't know how ugly I am? You think I don't see when women get sick inside when they see me? You think I don't know what all your fancy friends think when they see me? I think about it all the time, Rooney. And every time I think about it, I hear you laughin' in the background. You got a real mean laugh, Rooney. And half the time you're fuckin' laughin' at *me*."

This time Tolan used his fist, hooking it up under Rooney's jaw, knocking him back flat on the bed. Now there would be a bruise through the line of blood Tolan had opened up.

"I'll tell you how it's gonna be, Rooney. You 'n' me are goin' to Denver together. I'm keepin' your money till we get there. I'm gonna take your gun. You won't have no weapon. And if you try anything on me, I swear I'll kill you on the spot."

"What about my money?" Rooney said, closing his eyes, apparently from the pain of Tolan's fist.

"When we get to Denver, you get half."

"Half? What the hell're you talking about, half?" He came up off the bed angry. Rage had revived him. "Half? Bullshit."

"Half. Or nothing. Up to you."

"Why the hell should you get half?"

"Well, for one reason because you wouldn't give me even half if you were in my place. So I'm being generous. And for another reason, the money I take from you should clear us for all the money you stole from me over the years."

"Half," Rooney said. "You sonofabitch." Then, bitterly and to himself: "Half."

"It's up to you."

"So you're with me till train time?"

"You ain't gettin' out of my sight."

"Maybe you'll change your mind, Tolan. Maybe you'll start thinking more clearly."

The bad teeth once again. "I wouldn't bet on it, Rooney."

CHAPTER NINETEEN

Prine and Neville reached Junction Gap at eight o'clock that night. A light, cold mist gave the town an ominous look. Ground fog was up to the hips.

On the trail, they'd debated whether to ask the local law for help. They'd decided against it. Get the local law involved and somebody would immediately start thinking about the reward. And the prospect of all that money would make them secretive rather than cooperative. They'd fix it up so a friend or relative of theirs made the arrest and could claim the reward.

They found the livery stable. Their animals deserved food and a rest. It'd been a difficult trek. Not only the terrain. They'd been running the horses fast and hard. They described Tolan and Neville, but the liveryman didn't recall seeing such a pair.

" 'Course, Junction City, an awful lot of people come and go," the liveryman said. "You'd best try the saloons and the hotels. That's where most fellas end up when they come here."

Prine remembered something. "You got a roster?"

"Roster?" The moon-faced man wore a sheepskin, had a red scarf wrapped around his neck several times, sported heavy blue earmuffs, and had his hands snugged into mittens. The temperature was still in the low thirties. Prine wondered what the man wore when deep winter came. Maybe he didn't leave his house.

"A list. All the horses you put up today."

"Say, I never thought of that."

The liveryman led them back to a cubbyhole with a desk and two rickety wooden chairs. There was no escaping the acid smell of horse dung. In a confined space like this livery, the stench could make your eyes sting and water.

"Here you go."

Plain piece of paper. Date at the top. Nine names had been entered today. Tolan and Rooney wouldn't be foolish enough to put down their real names. The earliest they could have gotten here was just after dawn. The trouble was, the names weren't accompanied by the time a given horse was brought in.

"That help you any?" the liveryman said.

"Afraid not. Well, thanks. Guess we'll be going."

"I sure don't envy you goin' out on a night like this one," the liveryman said, huddling down into his sheepskin and batting his mittened hands together. "Like to freeze your tail off."

"Yeah," Prine said, "and just wait till it gets down into the twenties."

They went to the railroad station.

"Wish I could help you fellas," said the middle-aged man at the ticket counter. "But I just come on here a while ago. You'd want Vance. He works the seven-to-three shift. He might be able to help you."

"When's the next train due in here?"

"Supposed to be about an hour from now. But we got a telegram sayin' they're runnin' a little late. Some cattle got on the tracks. Lucky the train stayed upright. You run into four or five beeves when you're doin' sixty, you got some fine mess on your hands."

The ticket agent yawned every two minutes or so. And got both Prine and Neville yawning, too. Any other time and circumstance, Prine would've found this pretty funny.

"How many hotels in town here?" Prine said.

"Four."

"They all on the main street?"

"Yep. Two on the same little block, in fact. Good place for you fellas to put in for the night. A real friendly place, Junction Gap."

As they walked away from the railroad station, Neville said, "We could always sit here and wait for them to come to us."

"I was thinking of that, too," Prine said. "But what if they change their minds and decide to go on horseback? We'd be sitting in that railroad station a long time."

"Well, since there are four hotels, you take two and I'll take two. How's that?"

"Fine." Prine searched the misty gloom. The lights in The Good Meal Café promised warmth and a full belly and relaxation. He could easily imagine him sitting in there, taking it easy. After this was all over, that would be his first stop.

"All right," Prine said. "And if we don't turn anything up, we meet back here in an hour."

"If we don't turn anything up, I'm going to be damned disappointed," Neville said.

As Neville started to turn away, Prine grabbed the sleeve of his sheepskin and said, "You just remember our agreement. We want to take them back alive. Sheriff Daly'll have a lot of questions for them."

"I'll remember that," Neville said. "And

you remember that Cassie was my sister and that I loved her more than I've ever loved anybody." He pushed Prine's hand away from his sleeve. "I'll abide by the law, Prine. But if I find them and they give me any grief, I don't make any promises."

"That's fair enough," Prine said.

And with that, they set off to start searching the hotels.

Prine checked the saloons on his way to the hotels. He didn't see Tolan. He asked the various bartenders but found himself up against the bartenders' code of silence. Prine reasoned that all saloons should have a sign that said "Bullshit Spoken Here" up behind the bar. It would save lawmen, wives, and process servers a whole lot of time.

The one bartender who claimed to have knowledge of such men said that he wanted ten dollars for the information. The sly way he said it told Prine that this man, too, was speaking the universal bartender language of bullshit.

The first hotel he tried had a desk clerk who couldn't quite make up his mind if Tolan was there or not, a twitchy little man in a celluloid collar that left raw chafe marks around his chicken neck.

"The way you describe him," he said to Prine, "it sounds like he could be the man in 201."

"I'll check it out."

"On the other hand, the way you describe him sounds like he could also be the man in 111."

"They look sort of alike, huh?"

"Sort of. But then, the man in 206 also looks a little like the way you describe him."

"Looks like I'm going to be busy."

"But last week — last week we had a man that looked *exactly* like him."

"Last week Tolan would've been in Claybank."

"Well, I guess I didn't mean *exactly*, anyway, come to think of it. This Tolan, he doesn't have a limp and a glass eye, does he?"

"I don't think so."

"Well, then it wouldn't have been the man in here last week, anyway. He looked exactly as you described Tolan except —"

"— except for the glass eye and the limp."

"Right. Exactly."

Prine sighed and started checking up on rooms 201, 111, and 206.

The problem was, Prine decided when

the door to 201 was opened, the desk clerk shouldn't be so vain about wearing his glasses. Big, thick glasses. And he was apparently so blind that he should wear them twenty-four hours a day. Even when he slept.

The man who opened 201 was a scrawny redhead with a cigar jammed into the corner of his mouth and a half-naked woman on his bed. She was rubbing her crotch. Hard to tell if the rubbing was for pleasure or because she had a disease.

"Yeah?" the man said.

"Sorry to bother you. Looking for somebody else."

The guy nodded to the woman behind him on the bed.

"I finally get her to go along and you have to come knockin'?"

"I'm sorry."

"You can stuff your sorry as far as I'm concerned," the man said.

And he slammed the door.

The man who opened the door at 206 was at least fifty years old, bald, and was in the process of hawking up enough phlegm to fill a reservoir.

"What the hell you want?" he snapped between green gooey snorts.

"I must have the wrong room."

"I'm snufflin' my guts up and you have the wrong room? Get the hell outta here."

He caught 111 when he went back downstairs.

The man who opened this one was in a wheelchair. He was fortyish, gray-haired, and looked both intelligent and friendly.

"Wrong room, I guess. Sorry."

"Nothing to be sorry for. I appreciate the company. My granddad owns this place and just gives me this room. I'm in here all day trying to write a novel. And then at night I just sit at the window and look out at the street. I'd like to be up on the second floor. I'd have a better view."

"I just got the wrong room is all," Prine said, uncomfortable around the man in the wheelchair and feeling guilty because he *was* uncomfortable. "I'm really sorry to intrude."

"Say, if you're down in the saloon and somebody wants to have a party, send 'em up here."

"Your granddad wouldn't mind?"

"He used to mind when I had parties here. But he hasn't complained since they buried him about four months ago." The man had a big, sad smile on his face.

Not that Prine had any better luck at the next hotel. According to the chunky blond

German fellow behind the desk — a very jolly man was he, except for the killer eyes — there had never been, in the history of this particular hotel, anybody who even remotely fit the description of this Tolan man. For one thing, this Tolan man, said the clerk, sounded far too common to stay in a hotel of such obvious prestige. For another thing, this Tolan man would have instantly attracted the attention of Heinrich, the former Pinkerton man who now worked as the hotel detective. And for a final thing, this man would not even have come here because he would've heard that the hotel prices would make it impossible. He said all this with great pride.

Leaving Prine back on the street.

Leaving him to wonder how Neville was doing.

Leaving him to wonder if they'd find Tolan and Rooney in time.

"You go get the sheriff, you think there's gonna be any trouble," the desk clerk told Robert Neville.

"There won't be any trouble."

"That's what you say now. How do I know you get up there and there won't be a shoot-out?"

The desk clerk was a heavyset man who

268

kept a handkerchief on the desk to daub his face with. His face looked as if it had been glazed. His brown shirt was soaked around the collar and in the armpits.

"I don't want a shoot-out."

"That don't mean they won't give you one."

At this point, Neville reached for what he'd reached for all his life. His wallet. He took a considerable number of greenbacks from the wallet and laid them on the counter.

"What's that for?" the desk clerk asked.

"You really don't know what that's for?"

"Look, mister, that money looks nice now. But what about when it's gone and I lose my job? You want to explain that to my wife and three kids? I need a job a lot more than I need that money."

Neville laid more greenbacks on top of the counter.

"You must really want them two."

He kept staring at the money.

"I do."

"You mind I ask why?"

"Yeah, I do mind. It's none of your business."

But even as he spoke harshly, he laid more greenbacks on the counter.

"I still think you should go get the sheriff

and have him help you."

Four more greenbacks were laid down.

"Pretty soon, I'm going to pick up my money and go home."

The clerk ran a pudgy finger around his collar.

"I could really get in trouble here, mister. I ain't just sayin' that."

"Think how your wife's eyes will light up when you bring all this money home."

The clerk smiled. "Yeah, she'd be happy, all right." A frown quickly erased the smile. "But she'd be scared."

"Of what?"

"Of Mr. Peck findin' out I took this money."

"Maybe I should talk to Mr. Peck."

"Can't."

"Why not?"

"He's in California."

"Then how the hell's he ever going to find out?"

The expression in the clerk's brown gaze altered without any words being spoken. He must've been thinking of making his wife happy again, because he broke into a smile that would win him a smile contest at the county fair.

"You're right," the clerk said, sweeping the money on the counter up with a massive hand. "Now, you promise no rough stuff?"

"No rough stuff."

"And you promise no gunplay?"

"No gunplay. Just give me the room numbers," Neville said with increasing impatience, "and let me get on with my business."

With an important sigh — the things I have to do to make a living, the clerk's sigh said — he leaned forward, took a blank sheet of paper, a No. 3 lead pencil, and wrote down the two room numbers.

Neville hitched up his holster and set off for the stairs.

CHAPTER TWENTY

"It ain't gonna work," Tolan said.

"What isn't going to work?" Rooney said.

"You think I'll get drunk and pass out and then you'll take all the money and run."

"Our train'll be here in two hours or so. That wouldn't be enough time to get you that drunk."

They were in Tolan's room. Tolan had checked Rooney for weapons before letting him come in and sit down. Rooney had brought a bottle of rye with him. It had sat, unopened, for nearly an hour now.

Tolan nodded at the bottle. "That's a nice bottle."

"I figured we'd have ourselves a nice little drink before we left. We've been friends a long time, Tolan."

"We've never been friends, Rooney. You're too selfish to have friends. You even left me behind when I was wounded."

"You would've left me."

Tolan eyed him and shook his head.

"That's the funny thing, Rooney. I wouldn't have. I would've been dumb enough to find you a horse and take you with me."

Rooney smiled that cold, cold smile. "You're a sentimental man, Tolan. Nobody'd think you were, if they just met you and all." The smile vanished. "But it's dangerous, Tolan. Being sentimental like that. It gives other people a weapon against you."

"You left me, and even so I took up with you again."

"Nobody forced you, Tolan."

"And you kept on screwing me every way you could. A little bit here and a little bit there. But it all added up."

"I thought we'd have a friendly drink before train time, Tolan."

"I'm like that poor old collie we had on the farm. The old man'd get drunk and try and teach it tricks, but the dog never picked up on 'em very good. And so the old man'd beat her and beat her with his razor strop. He'd draw blood. He even put one of her eyes out. My little sister 'n' me'd cry and beg my old man to stop hitting the dog. But he never would. He'd go beating her until he got bored and turned on one of us. The funny thing was that we were just like that collie. No matter how much the old man'd beat us, we forgive him. We loved him. There wasn't any reason to love him. But we loved him just like that poor old collie did. I guess that's what you mean by sentimental, huh, Rooney?"

But Rooney's mind was elsewhere. He'd never taken any interest in Tolan's trouble, and he clearly wasn't about to start now.

Without warning, Tolan picked up the bottle of rye and tossed it to Rooney. Rooney caught it with his crotch. He laughed. "You could've caused some permanent damage there."

Tolan didn't smile. "You take the first drink."

"Tolan, God Almighty, you think I put something in this drink."

"I sure do."

"You're too smart for something like that. I wouldn't even try it."

Tolan sat up on the bed, pointing the six-shooter at Rooney's head.

"Take a drink, Rooney."

"I just had a full meal. Don't really feel like drinking right now."

"You don't take a drink there, Rooney, I'm gonna kill you on the spot."

"Now, that wouldn't make a lot of sense, would it?"

"Sure it would. I'm pretty dumb, but I can sure make it look like you fired at me first. I might spend a night or two in a cell. But a good lawyer'd get me off. And I'd still have plenty of money left to go to California." Tolan pulled the hammer back. "Now, go on, Rooney, and take a drink."

"Aw, shit," Rooney said. Then he laughed — almost giggled, in fact, like a tyke who'd been caught stealing something from his old man's coin box. "I might as well admit it."

"Yeah. You might as well."

"I queered the rye."

"You prick. I knew that's what you done."

Rooney pitched the bottle on the bed.

"You took my money, Tolan. What the hell else could I do?"

"I thought you said I was too smart to go for queering the drink."

The icy smile. "Well, you didn't go for it, did you? But I still thought I'd give it a try anyway."

Tolan was about to say something when they heard heavy footsteps in the hall. And then a heavy knock.

Tolan and Rooney glanced at each other.

"Who is it?" Tolan said, not moving from the bed.

"Sheriff's office. Deputy McBride."

This time when they glanced at each, there was tension in their eyes. Somebody from the sheriff's office wasn't what they needed with less than two hours to go until train time.

"What is it you need?" Rooney said.

"Sheriff wants me to ask you a couple questions. This won't take long."

Tolan started up from the bed, his gun aimed directly at the door. He holstered that and picked up a sawed-off.

Rooney half-leapt at Tolan, grabbing the man's gun wrist, pushing against the sawed-off.

Rooney whispered: "We sure as hell don't want a shoot-out. Let's just see what he wants. Maybe they just like to hassle strangers here."

With that, Rooney shrugged and tugged his suit into proper fitting position, slicked back his hair with the palms of both hands, and then wiped a heavy finger across his lips, in case he'd left some crumbs there.

He looked back at Tolan. Tolan was ready to reenact the Civil War right here and right now. That was all he knew how to do.

But this situation called for a civilized man of intelligence and self-control. One who could, through charm and subterfuge, make short order of a hick deputy sheriff.

He opened the door, and Richard Neville hit him in the face with the butt of a Sharps buffalo rifle.

Rooney — not a tough man, not a tough man at all — went wheeling backward, a womanly sound emitting from his lips.

Tolan tried to reach his sawed-off, but it was too late for that now, wasn't it?

Neville closed the door behind him and said, "You two were supposed to be on a steamboat two days ago. God knows I paid you two enough money to take care of my sister and then get away from here. What the hell happened?"

Chapter Twenty-one

There was a lot of disagreement from people in the hotel — staff and guests alike — as to which came first: the sound of the Colt or the sound of the sawed-off. Opinion seemed to divide right down the middle.

The sheriff's name was Walt Naismith. He was tall, sinewy, and carried a wad of chaw that made his cheek look eight months pregnant. He wore a dusty suit and a suspicious expression.

He checked it all out upstairs, where the killings had taken place, meanwhile keeping Neville in the temporary custody of a lone deputy in the lobby.

The gunfire hadn't been difficult to hear. Prine had been less than a block away when it came. He knew who was involved. What he didn't know then was who had survived.

Now he sat next to Neville in the hotel café, across the table from Naismith, who had dragged a spittoon over to his chair.

"These the men killed your sister?" Naismith said.

"Yes, sir, they are," Neville said.

"And you're sure of that?"

"Yes, I am, Sheriff. And the deputy here will vouch for me."

"Is that true, son? You'll vouch for him?"

"If you're asking me were these the men who killed his sister, yes. I believe they were."

"And you don't have any reason *not* to believe they were?"

"I guess I don't follow."

Naismith smiled around his chaw.

"Not fun when you're the one being asked the questions. You're too used to bein' the asker instead of the askee."

"That's probably right. Hadn't thought of it that way."

"What I'm getting at here, son, is do you have any major doubt about them bein' the killers?"

"None that I can think of."

"Good, son. Now back to you, Mr. Neville. And let me say that I'm well aware of who you are and who your pop was. But I treat all people fair and square — at least most of them — so I'm not gonna go too easy on you or too hard. You understand?"

"I do, sir. But it's actually pretty simple, you see —"

"One thing I learned in thirty years of

bein' a lawman, nothin' is pretty simple. Not even the simple stuff is simple."

Neville sighed impatiently, sat back in his chair, and folded his arms like a man whose wife had dragged him to a ballet.

"I'm glad to answer any of your questions," he told Naismith.

"Very good. That's the way we need to handle this. That way we can speed things right along." He sipped his coffee. Then spat. "Now, did you ever see Tolan and Rooney before today?"

"No, I didn't."

"How did you know they were in those rooms?"

Neville explained how he'd worked all the saloons and hotels.

"Did the deputy warn you about getting violent with them?"

"Yes, he did. He was very explicit about it. He said that just because they'd killed my sister didn't give me any right to kill them unless it was in self-defense."

"And you're saying that it was self-defense?"

"Oh, absolutely it was. Tolan — that's the dark one, that's the only way I can keep them apart in my head — Tolan let me in, but then he only gave me about a minute before he brought up the sawed-off and fired at me."

"Two bullets, from what I can see, Mr. Neville."

"That's right, he fired twice."

"Did Rooney shoot at you?"

"He certainly did. Twice also, I believe. It looked like an old Colt to me."

Naismith looked at Prine.

"You ever hear of that, son? A man with a six-shooter like Mr. Neville's here holding off a man with a sawed-off and another man with a six-shooter?"

Prine shrugged his shoulders.

"In my experience, you can never predict how a shoot-out like that is going to go. There're a lot things involved. Speed, accuracy, courage — you just can't predict."

Naismith turned back to Neville.

"So there you were and you were facing two armed men. And what did you do?"

"About the only thing I could. I threw myself in front of the bed and crouched down. There wasn't a lot of space."

"You fired from that position?"

"Yes."

"Do you remember who you fired at first?"

"I'm pretty sure it was Rooney. He was closest to me."

"Do you remember where you hit him?"

"It's all a blur. But I remember afterward — when he was down on the floor, I mean — I remember seeing this large dark hole in his forehead."

"How did you come to shoot Tolan?"

"He had to reload. And I heard him. I told him I wouldn't fire on him if he gave himself up."

"So you warned him?"

"Yes. I thought of what Prine here told me. About how I could fire only in self-defense."

"So there he is reloading, and you shot him?"

"He had a pistol underneath his blanket. He pulled it on me and . . ."

"And you shot him."

"Yes."

"Do you remember where you wounded him?"

"The chest, I believe."

"The chest and the face."

"Yes. Then I just got out of the room as soon as I could. I needed to get out in the hallway. Fresh air. I was getting sick to my stomach. Maybe I did hit him in the face, too."

"I'll be honest with you here, Mr. Neville," Naismith said. "We're not a rich county, and you could put up one hell of a fight that we'd probably lose anyway. Prine here knows what I'm talking about."

"You're not saying what you mean, Naismith," Prine said.

"I'm not saying he's guilty."

"But you're not saying he's innocent, either."

Naismith sighed and shrugged. "My boys talked to the people staying in the room next to Tolan's room. They heard the shooting, but they didn't hear anything else. And that might mean that they actually didn't hear anything or that they know who your friend Neville is and they don't want to get involved. Either way, all they heard was the shots. They don't know who started the fight or who fired first. We checked all the guests on that floor to see if anybody was walking past the door and heard anybody in Tolan's room talking. There were five people on the floor at that time, or so they say, and not one of them heard anything. Or so they say."

"So you'll have to take Neville's word for it," Prine said.

"This isn't the old days," Naismith said. "We're all legaled up now, or like to think we are. You get two men dead and you're talking to the man who killed them, you hope you can get some kind of corroboration for what he's saying."

"I guess his word's about all you've got."

"Then I can go? I want to get back home, Sheriff."

Naismith smiled. "I needed to put a little fear in you, Neville, feel like I was doin' my job at least a little bit."

Neville's smile was one of those big public smiles that politicians hand out like promises.

"Well, for what it's worth, you got my stomach in knots for a few minutes there, Sheriff."

"Good," Naismith said, offering a large, worn, liver-spotted chunk of hand. "Now I'll sleep better tonight."

Chapter Twenty-two

By the time they reached the town limits of Claybank, mist and fog had turned them into cold, unspeaking wraiths. They'd each nodded off from time to time. Hard to say who was more tired, the men or their horses.

"I'll be turning off here," Neville said. His face was slick with moisture. He stank of grime and sleep and dampness. "You're going to say no to this, Prine. But I don't want you to. I'll consider it an insult if you do, in fact. I'm drawing a check for a thousand dollars for you and having somebody from the bank run it over to the sheriff's office tomorrow."

"I wish you wouldn't."

"After all we went through? You sure as hell earned it."

"I was doing my job is all."

"You need more satisfaction than that."

"What sort've satisfaction will you get? Cassie's dead."

Even through the mist, Neville's smile was clear and clean.

"I got the satisfaction of killing them."

"Naismith's right," Prine said. "I guess you're the only one who'll ever know if you killed those two in cold blood."

"For what it's worth, Prine, I didn't."

"I'm glad to know that." He cinched his hat lower on his head and said, "Well, good night, then."

"Good night, Prine. And remember, you're to cash that check." Neville swung away and disappeared into the murk.

An hour later, Prine, in long johns, with a cup of coffee in one hand and a cigarette in the other, sat in his bed feeling that the past couple days just might have been a dream. Or nightmare, actually.

Everything had happened too quickly to be understood in any comprehensible way. A girl was kidnapped, murdered, he and Neville had pursued the killers, and the killers had died trying to kill Neville, or they had died when Neville executed them. At this moment, Prine really didn't give much of a damn which way it had happened.

He'd sent Sheriff Daly a long telegram ahead indicating that Tolan and Rooney's bodies would be shipped back to Claybank by train in a day or so and that both he and Neville were tired but otherwise all right.

Now all he needed to do was relax and sleep.

When he realized that he was going over and over everything as a means of not facing what really worried him — telling Daly the truth about his plan to take advantage of the kidnapping and play the hero — he stubbed out his smoke and set his coffee on the floor next to the bed.

If he was going to brood on that, it might as well be in the dark, where he just might have a chance of getting tired enough to sleep.

As he walked to work in the morning, still tired from the past couple of days, Prine worked on the way he would approach Daly this morning. Bob Carlyle generally went to the café first, and that was around ten. He took fifteen, twenty minutes. This would be all the time Prine would have alone with Daly — if Daly wasn't called away or some unexpected trouble didn't take both of them from the office.

He'd say, *I made a bad mistake, Sheriff. And I need to talk to you about it.* He half-smiled about this. It would be like going to confession. That's exactly what he'd be doing this morning. He'd say the rest the same way — straight out. He wouldn't make any excuses. There were no excuses to be made. Then it would be up to Daly.

Just before Prine reached the sheriff's office, his stomach curdled and the rolling jitters passed up and down his arms. This sure as hell wasn't going to be easy.

"There he is now," Daly's voice said before Prine had even crossed the threshold.

A city man in a homburg and a dark blue suit stood, holding a briefcase. He was a formal, stiff-looking man of forty years or so. If he'd ever laughed, you couldn't prove it by his narrow, severe face or hard blue judgmental eyes.

Bob Carlyle was grabbing his hat. Daly walked over and yanked his off the peg, too. "Prine, this is Mr. Silas Beaumont. Remember Al Woodward, who was here investigating the Pentacle fire? Well, he still hasn't turned up. So Mr. Beaumont here, who's a vice president of the insurance company Woodward hired out to, is here to find Woodward and carry on with the arson investigation. I told him that you'd talked to Aaron Duncan and that you'd be glad to help him. Meanwhile, Carlyle here and I thought we'd grab us a cup of coffee."

It was almost comical, the way Daly and

Carlyle were rushing out the door. The Mr. Silas Beaumonts of the world were difficult to deal with. They just assumed, you being small-town, you were stupid and probably corrupt.

"See you soon, Mr. Beaumont," Daly said as he half-dove through the door, slamming it hard shut behind him.

"Coffee, Mr. Beaumont?"

"I'm not here for a chat, Mr. Prine. At this moment, I should be in Lincoln, Nebraska, where the stockholders of our company are holding their annual meeting. Instead, I'm in your little burg trying to find out what happened to one of our freelance investigators. There's a train out of here this evening, and I hope to be on it. So no — no coffee, no chat, nothing extraneous. If I can get on that train this evening, then I can be in Lincoln in a day and a half. Still time to pay my respects to our stockholders."

No coffee? How about a cob to shove up your ass? Prine thought. He'd gone from a reasonably good mood — hoping Daly would understand and forgive him — to a dour one thanks to this pale, mannequinlike intruder who was as imperious as a well-connected politician.

Prine said, "Well, I'll have a cup for

myself, if you don't mind."

As he was pouring his coffee, he said, "When's the last time you heard from Woodward?"

"Last week."

"He pretty reliable, is he?"

"We check our freelancers out thoroughly."

Prine, steaming coffee in hand, angled his bottom onto the edge of his desk. He kicked a chair with rollers on it over to Beaumont. Beaumont's bloodless lips pinched up in displeasure. He wasn't going to give this office a very good grade. Not that Prine gave a damn.

But Beaumont sat down, briefcase on lap.

"Do you know anything about Aaron Duncan, Mr. Prine?"

Prine shrugged. "That he used to be a successful businessman is about all I know."

"Used to be?"

"The last recession hit everybody out here pretty hard. Farm prices went to hell, and the railroad didn't make us a spur the way they'd originally promised. Most people were in a bad way."

"From what I'm able to gather, Aaron Duncan owns four businesses within a one-hundred-mile radius."

Prine sipped some coffee. "That, I didn't know. Then maybe the recession didn't hit him as hard as it did some others."

"Or maybe it did. This is the third business — the Pentacle mattress factory — to be destroyed by fire."

"I see," Prine said. And he did. "Did you pay off on the other two?"

"Yes."

"Nothing suspicious about them?"

"A lot suspicious about them. But nothing we could prove."

"But this time —"

"Three out of four businesses owned by one man go up in smoke? The probability is virtually zero."

"He sounds desperate."

"Desperate and sloppy. The last time we heard from Al Woodward was in a wire he sent. He said he was sure he could prove arson at Pentacle."

Prine remembered talking to Aaron Duncan a few days ago. How Duncan's wife had left the office angrily, following an argument of some kind. He also remembered the bartender saying that Woodward had been looking at a letter somebody sent him. Would Aaron Duncan's wife — if she was angry enough — cooperate with

Woodward by sending him a note?

"Do you have any ideas, Deputy?"

"One. Maybe." He told Beaumont what he'd seen in Duncan's office, the wife so furious when she left.

"It could have been about anything — their argument, I mean."

"I agree. But I still think it'd be worth talking to Mrs. Duncan."

Beaumont didn't look happy. "Anything else?"

Beaumont's disappointment irritated Prine. Made him defensive. Maybe Mrs. Duncan wasn't such a great idea. But she was a better idea than Beaumont had.

Beaumont said, "You checked all the —"

"— hotels, saloons, boardinghouses. No trace of Woodward."

Beaumont stood up. "I have a meeting in twenty minutes with Aaron Duncan. Maybe I'll have a little more luck with him than you do. I'm a pretty good interrogator, if I do say so myself. In the big cities, knowing how to question a man and lead him into a verbal trap is a valued skill. We used to do what you do out here — just beat a man till he talks — but we've found a skilled interrogation to be much more useful."

"I don't beat the men I question," Prine

said. "I usually set them on fire."

"My Lord," said Beaumont, "is that true?"

Prine smiled. "No. But you wouldn't have been surprised, would you, Mr. Beaumont? The way lawmen treat prisoners 'out here.'"

Beaumont looked both unhappy and uncomfortable as he made his way to the front door. As if Prine had suddenly revealed himself to be a mental defective of some kind. What sort of person made jokes about setting other people on fire?

Most disturbing, most disturbing, Beaumont was obviously thinking, as he put his hand on the doorknob and made a hasty departure.

CHAPTER TWENTY-THREE

There was a young woman Prine had briefly dated when he'd come to Claybank. She worked in the county records office. Prine had been more interested in her than she'd been in him. After a few evenings of stilted courting, she admitted that she was sorry but that she was just using his good looks as a way of making another young man jealous enough to ask her to marry him.

Which had apparently worked, because slender Sharon Sullivan was now portly and with child as she waddled up to him behind the counter of the records office. "Hi, Tom." She smiled. "I weigh a little more than the last time you saw me."

"Well, congratulations."

"Thanks." Even with a fleshy face, her smile radiated the pride of a good and decent woman. "And Art wants another one right after this."

"I'm glad it all worked out for you, Sharon."

Her sweet face tightened. "I'm just sorry I wasn't nicer to you."

"It was fine," he said. "And it turned out fine, too."

They talked a few more minutes about people they knew in common. This was the age — she was twenty-four to Prine's twenty-nine — that most still-unmarried folks, men and women alike, started looking around for a lifelong mate. There was plenty of gossip about all those various couplings and uncouplings.

Finally, he said, "You've got the records of local businesses, don't you?"

"Depends what you mean by 'records.'"

"You know. Who started them. Then who bought them. And then if there are any silent partners."

"Oh, sure. We'd have that on just about every business in the valley. Who're you looking for?"

"Pentacle Mattresses."

She laughed. "We've been so busy around here, I haven't even had time to put it away. It's sitting on my desk right now."

"Oh? Somebody else asked to see it?"

"Man named Woodward. Insurance investigator is what he said."

"When was this?"

"Let me think." She had a pert little freckled nose that was fun to gaze upon.

And gaze he did. "Monday, I guess." She patted the belly beneath her blue gingham dress. "I wasn't feeling too good. You know how women get in the morning. He was telling me how his wife had gotten with their four kids. He seemed like a nice fella. He still around town?"

"That's what we're trying to find out." He told her about Beaumont and Woodward missing. "Can people just ask to see the file?"

"Afraid not, Tom. We can look up things for them, but we can't just hand the files over." Her smile made her small, exquisite face — so nicely framed with hair the color of mahogany — look like a drawing of a woman in a magazine. "But I forgot. You're a deputy. All you have to do is sign a form and I can turn the file over to you."

"Knew there was a reason I wore this badge," he said. "So I can throw my weight around in the records office."

"Be right back," she said.

He spent fifteen minutes with the file, sitting in a chair in a corner like a boy who'd misbehaved in class. People came in and out, looking at his seat outside the counter. They probably wondered what a deputy was doing looking through a file. They also probably thought that something pretty interesting was going on. This was, after all, the deputy who'd gone looking for Cassie Neville.

Everything in the files was routine. As the state required, there was about half a pound of various legal documents establishing Aaron Duncan and a company named River's Edge properties as co-owners of the mattress-manufacturing firm. There was no information at all on River's Edge except a post office box address in the state capital. The signatures for River's Edge had been entered by the attorney, whose address was also listed as being in the state capital. Did this mean the signature was a legal proxy or that the lawyer himself was River's Edge and therefore signing for the company?

He asked Sharon about this.

"I really can't say, Tom. I'm sure the owner's name has to be on file somewhere. Maybe it is this lawyer."

He wrote down the name River's Edge and the number of the post office box. He pushed the file back to her and said, "Good luck with the kid."

"It's good seeing you again, Tom. Hopefully next time, I'll be a little thinner."

"You look great."

She'd wanted reassurance that she was

still an appealing woman — which she definitely was — and Prine was happy to give it to her.

Five minutes later, he was at the telegraph office, writing out the message he wanted sent to the River's Edge attorney in the state capital.

That afternoon, Cassie Neville was buried.

The town had never seen such a crowd of important people. You knew they were important because of the way they strode about, the way they ordered lesser humans about, and the way they would tell you they were important if you failed to recognize their splendiferous humanity. Even the governor attended, taking time to do his usual politicking, of course. He probably had chapped lips from all the kissing he did. He made short order of the babies, but lingered longer bussing the mothers.

The interior of the church was so crowded with flowers that several people had allergic reactions. There was a lot of sneezing.

When Richard Neville, godlike once more, made his shining way up the center aisle of the church, everyone turned to look at him. Would he cry? Would he come apart? Or — wouldn't this be pretty remarkable — would he faint? Bereaved men had been known to faint at the funerals of their loved ones. Imagine someone as big and strong and handsome as Richard Neville, the richest man in this part of the state, crumpling in his pew, while someone rushed for smelling salts and a piece of cloth dipped in cool water?

He didn't do any of those things, of course.

He took his seat in the front pew with the other close relatives and sat there with his hands on his knees for the entire ceremony. He didn't look around, he didn't speak, he didn't sing when the others opened their hymnals.

He wasn't much different at graveside. He watched it all with stern mien but didn't seem to be participating in the communal mourning. He looked as if he had other business to attend to. But since Cassie's killers were dead, people couldn't imagine what that other business would be.

One of the horses pulling the hearse played wild for a few minutes, frightening some children. The minister reading the services developed a cough he couldn't seem to quell for long. And Mrs. Morgan, who had moved here with her brood only a month before and had in fact never laid eyes on Cassie except in the coffin, wept so extravagantly that some people began to smirk at her. My Lord, was she auditioning for some kind of play?

The temperature stayed at a sunny sixty-five. Autumn had never looked lovelier than it did right now.

Every once in a while, Prine had the impulse to step in front of the coffin and explain that she might still be alive if it hadn't been for his stupid plan to get rich. But he was too shy to do this. He would be a ridiculous figure, making a public confession that way. Living with guilt was bad enough; purposely making yourself a figure of foolishness was even harder to bear.

In town, Prine went directly to the telegraph office.

The lawyer for River's Edge, a Mr. Kyle Abernathy, had already wired back.

CO-OWNER OF PENTACLE
MATTRESS
CONFIDENTIAL INFORMATION.
SORRY.
WOULD NEED COURT ORDER.

He'd expected this. Lawyers weren't about to give out client information of this nature without a battle. That's what people paid lawyers for — protection.

He went over to the bank to see Eugene Sims. Sims had a nineteen-year-old son who'd been born with a hand the shape of a bottle — a whiskey bottle. You rarely saw that hand when it wasn't that shape. Todd Sims was always getting into trouble of the public intoxication kind. Prine always ran the kid home instead of charging him and putting him in jail. This wasn't because Prine felt all that sorry for the young man, which he did to a small degree. It was because a bank vice president was somebody good to know. You never knew when a bank VP would come in handy.

Eugene Sims was a fleshy man with a round pink face and dog-sad brown eyes. He looked afraid when he saw Prine walking toward his desk in the back of the bank. There was only one enclosed office here, and that, needless to say, belonged to the bank president.

"Todd in trouble?" Sims asked, touching his tight, white celluloid collar.

"Relax, Eugene. Todd's fine."

Sims's relief was visible. He had his left hand on his desk. It was trembling. "Sit down, Tom. Since this visit doesn't involve my son, I can relax now. So what can I help you with, my friend?"

"You do Aaron Duncan's banking, right?"

"Yes, we're very glad to have him as a customer."

Prine leaned forward, giving the conversation an air of secrecy. "There's a co-owner for his mattress company."

"There is? Gosh, Sam, I handle that account myself. You sure about that?"

Prine nodded. "I wondered if you could check in his file and find the name of the other owner for me."

Sims leaned back. Talked around his steepled fingers. "You start looking through a man's personal files — it's not good, Tom."

"This is official business," Prine said.

"He in trouble?"

"Not that I know of. We're just trying to wrap up this investigation, and we need to know who all the players are."

"Then why don't you just ask Aaron Duncan himself?"

Prine was careful about what he said. "I'm trying to help Aaron. Keep his name clear of what could be a financial scandal. And lose him one hell of a lot of money. And prestige."

"In other words, he won't cooperate."

"Well," Prine said, "I really haven't

asked him yet. But I'm saving that as a last resort."

Sims sighed, sat forward. Nodded to the bank president, Homer Styles, who was standing outside the teller windows talking with some of the customers. He was a courtly man, a southern man, and those who weren't put off by his southern accent were enchanted by it. For many Yankees as well as southerners, the Civil War had yet to end.

"You see Styles out there? Can you imagine what he'd do to me if I gave you confidential information? I'd be out of a job, Tom. I just can't do it. The only way you could get it that I know of is to get a court order, and then you'd still have to deal with Styles, not me."

Prine shrugged. "I figured that's what you'd say. But I thought I'd give it a try."

"I'd help you if I could, Tom."

"Yeah, I know." He pushed himself up out of the chair. He'd always had a vague admiration for drummers. They could get turned down ten times a day and they could still find a reserve of enthusiasm to knock on one more door. Getting turned down drained him.

But as he walked out of the bank, his step quickened when he realized that there

303

was one more person he could try. A person who didn't seem to like Aaron Duncan all that much. Aaron Duncan's wife.

Richard Neville wondered if he could survive the late-afternoon gathering at his mansion. Another excuse for the local gentry to get drunk and stuff their bellies at his expense. And all the cloying, embarrassing speeches he had to endure. *She was so lovely. She was such a fine person. You must be so lonely. Anytime you feel like talking, just stop over. She would've wanted you to go on with your life, Richard.*

She'd been a stupid, whiny little bitch who'd wanted to be praised constantly for all the inane little things she did. My God, she never stopped bragging about her charity work; never stopped regaling him with tales of the boy-men who fell in love with her; and never talked about how she was going to give half of her fortune to charity.

What she hadn't known — few people did — was the catastrophic losses the business he'd inherited had suffered in the past few years. Against the advice of his lawyers, his accountants, and his bankers, he'd started buying up towns and hamlets rumored to have been chosen by railroads as railheads. He'd already squandered hundreds of thousands of dollars on bad cattle deals; on timberland that logging companies wouldn't meet his prices for; on a steamboat scheme that would've returned the rivers to their former majesty — despite the obvious fact that people preferred railroad travel these days. River travel was in terrible decline. All this was made even worse by the fact that he listened only to those cronies who agreed with him. Hell, he bought them drinks, food, women — why wouldn't they agree with him?

He'd managed to survive last year only because he'd been able to blackmail Aaron Duncan into letting him buy into Duncan's various businesses — and then destroy them. Neville had witnessed a drunken Duncan cut up a whore pretty badly one night — the woman almost bled to death before Neville, terrified of the scandal, called in a doc to take care of her. Duncan had no choice but to go along with Neville's arson plans. Neville got the cash flow he needed. But then the insurance company sent that damned Al Woodward out here. Neville sent him a note luring him to the lake and killed him there.

But he knew he was beyond the help of

arson. He needed a large amount of money, and he needed it quickly. That meant his sister's half of the family fortune.

He still remembered the day Rooney had come to Neville's buggy in town one day. The man even looked like a grifter, but it was easy to tell that Rooney thought otherwise. Rooney obviously saw himself as a very sleek-looking businessman. He would've ignored Rooney, but Rooney said, "I have some interesting news about your sister."

My God, you couldn't ask for a better opportunity. The stupid bitch had hired two lowlife grifters to kidnap her to teach big brother a lesson. Rooney offered to do whatever Neville said if the price was right. Neville made sure the price was right. He wanted Cassie murdered, and these scruffy boys were just the two to do it. He would make sure to kill them if he ever got the chance.

And he got his chance.

Now he watched all the hypocrites. They'd be laughing with their mouths and lusting with their eyes until it was their turn to come over and pay their respects to Richard. And then they would put on their grief masks. And natter on about what a loss she was. And how much he'd obviously loved her. And how, someday, he'd be able to carry on with his life.

He had a meeting on Monday with her lawyers. He needed to tap into her fortune, and quickly.

Chapter Twenty-four

The Duncan home had been built on a shelf above a leg of the river. Isolation and privacy were further provided by the fact that it had been built inside a sprawl of pine and pin oak trees so that it could not be seen from the road.

Prine's instinctive first response to this glimpse of the privileged life was one of unworthiness. He'd seen his old man roll over and grovel for rich people. He had the same shameful tendencies. You could try and convince yourself that all people were equal in the eyes of God and the law, but money bought power and power instilled fear. And fear . . .

By the time he dismounted, ground-tying his horse by the river, he felt less intimidated by the Victorian house looming up out of what had once been a prairie. The badge made him equal to anybody who lived here. He just needed to remember that.

Elenore Duncan came out the front door just as Prine reached the front steps. She wore an ice-blue frock that displayed her full but fetching body to advantage. Her hair was perfectly set, too, as if she might have been entertaining this afternoon. When she wobbled coming down the steps — he took her elbow just before she fell down — he realized that she'd been entertaining all right — herself. She was politely and properly drunk. She wasn't the first gentrified, middle-aged woman to suffer at the brutal hands of John Barleycorn.

"I saw you come up," she said. She flung a hand somewhere in the vicinity of the yard to the west. The grounds were elegantly landscaped and tended. Arson must pay better than I realized, Prine thought. "I love to sit in the gazebo. Come."

She slid her hand into his, as if they were teenage lovers. "Oh, God, I hate being sad all the time." She spoke to herself more than she did to him. "I used to sit by the window and wait and wait and wait for him to come home. Sometimes I'd sit up till nearly dawn. I didn't care about his gambling or his whores and all the stupid business deals he was always getting into. I just wanted him to come home to me."

Her hand still in his, she turned her face to him and for the first time he saw, beneath the excess flesh, the fine lyrical bones of the young woman she'd been. One of those wry, melancholy faces you could look at for hours. "And now you know what? Now I don't care if he ever comes home. In fact, I'd prefer if he'd stay away. Because when he's here, all we do is argue."

As they walked, her wide mouth became a full and appealing smile. "Have you guessed my secret yet, Deputy Prine?"

"I'm not sure, Mrs. Duncan."

"Oh, Lord. Don't make me feel older than I am. Please call me Ellie."

"My secret —" She stumbled. He seized her elbow again. She was still smiling when she stood straight again. "I think I just gave away my secret."

"You've been drinking."

"How observant. Are all deputies as observant as you are?"

"Yes. We take an oath to be observant."

"I'm drunk, Deputy Prine."

"Gosh, are you sure?"

She laughed.

"I like you. Do you like me?"

"Very much."

"You know something? My husband's afraid of you."

"Did he tell you that?"

"You paid him a visit the other day. I saw

you in his office. That Mr. Woodward scared him, too."

Prine was glad they weren't holding hands any longer. Because when she mentioned Woodward, his entire body tensed.

They reached the gazebo — classically shaped with a blue roof and white sides — and he helped her up the stairs and inside. They sat on a padded bench that allowed them to look at the river.

Prine rolled himself a cigarette. He was trying to figure out the best way to keep her talking.

"Did you ever meet Woodward?" he asked.

"Would you roll me one of those?"

"You smoke, huh?"

"Only when I'm drunk."

"Sure, I'll roll you one."

He rolled her one. Got it lit for her. Handed it to her. She knew how to smoke just fine. She looked good, too, inhaling, exhaling, cocking her head at a certain angle so that her long, fine neck was emphasized. The lips she'd just wetted sparkled with erotic promise.

She said, "Don't ask me to betray him."

"I assume we're talking about your husband."

"Yes, unfortunately — yes. All the times

and all the ways he's betrayed me. I don't know why I should give a damn about betraying him. I guess I still love him. That's the terrible thing about all this. I still love him."

He wondered if she was going to cry.

As soon as Aaron Duncan got the telegram, he said goodnight to his secretary and left Pentacle Mattress. It was barely 3:30.

He headed straight and fast to the Neville estate. He was trying to work up such an anger that not even Richard Neville could turn him aside. That was the hell of it with Neville. He was such a powerful man — both physically and because of his business reputation — that it was impossible for somebody like Duncan to take his verbal abuse. Like most people, Duncan always gave in to Neville, even when he knew he shouldn't. This time, at least, he was going to taunt him, say that Neville's idea for three arsons was stupid to begin with.

You don't think they'll catch on, Richard? You think insurance companies are dumb? Three businesses I own burn down in a four-month period and they don't have any suspicions? You're so desperate for money, you're not thinking straight, Richard. This third one — They'll catch us before. And this time, they're going to find out who my silent partner is, too. You wait and see. This time, they won't quit until they've found out everything.

Duncan had been drunk when he'd said all this one night in his office with Neville. Maybe that's what he needed now. The fortification, the wisdom of alcohol. But it was still the sunny afternoon. No way Neville would take him seriously if he showed up drunk.

The telegraph rode in his pocket like a coiled snake, ready to strike. His lawyer warning him that Prine had tried to get the name of Duncan's secret partner from him. Now it was both Prine and the insurance company moving in on them. And Neville kept on killing people. One dead in the mattress factory fire. Al Woodward the insurance investigator murdered. And in both of these, by law, Duncan had been complicit.

That first night when Neville had proposed it all, it all sounded so easy.

You need money, Aaron, and so do I. Your company's about three or four months from taking bankruptcy. I owe so much money, they may not even give me the regular bankruptcy protection. One thing's for sure — they'll take

313

*every single thing I own. Every single thing.
But I can lay my hands on just enough cash to
buy into your businesses and fix them up some.
Capital investment. My accountant'll doctor
the books so that it'll look like you're doing
very, very well for yourself. Then I hire somebody to burn the buildings down and we'll
split the proceeds.*

It had looked so easy.

The insurance company did only a cur-
sory examination of the first building.
They were naturally more curious — and
more deliberate — about number two.

Richard Neville went through his arson
money quickly, learning that it wasn't
enough to keep people off his back for
even a couple of weeks. So he'd proposed
arson number three. With a wrinkle.

*We'll make it look like somebody's got it in
for you, Aaron. We'll leave a note that says this
is fire number three. Fire number four'll be your
fancy new house. And we'll make it sound like
this arsonist's got some kind of grudge against
you. Maybe somebody you fired a long time
ago. Somebody who's really crazy, he hates you
so much. This way, it doesn't look like we had
anything to do with it. There's this maniac
running around. We can't help that, can we?*

Good ole Neville. The mastermind. The
genius. Just ask him.

Well, now he'd really have to be a mastermind. Obviously, the insurance company didn't believe the letter the "arsonist" left behind. And apparently neither did Prine, else why would he be firing off telegrams to Duncan's lawyer?

The estate was coming into view. Normally, sight of it would have made him feel better. There were always stiff drinks and good food to be had at the Neville mansion. Even listening to Richard brag wasn't so bad most of the time. Richard was an entertaining braggart. He had no sense of humor about himself, that was the biggest problem from a social standpoint. He couldn't detect his underlings gently laughing at him rather than with him. He couldn't tell a smirk from a smile.

But this afternoon, neither smirk nor smile would matter. All that counted was the telegram coiled in Duncan's pocket. With all the stress and strain Neville had been under lately, he was likely to go into one of his temper tantrums. These were truly terrifying and sickening spectacles. A grown man with no more control of himself than a spoiled seven-year-old. He'd curse, smash things, and then turn on whichever poor unfortunate had been designated to bring him the bad news. Killing the messenger was part of the fun for Richard — his eyes bugged out, his face scarlet with boiling blood, spittle flying like silver worms from his lips.

That was when you needed to stand up to him.

Duncan had to remember that. He was a full partner in all this. He was complicit in the murders of at least two people. He had the right to speak up and the right to be listened to with great seriousness.

Even if Richard *tried* to shut up him, Richard was going to by God listen to him. Even if Duncan had to put a gun to his head.

He was sick of Richard, sick of his life — and, most especially, sick of himself.

He rode through the open black wrought-iron gates leading to the dusty road that eventually wound past the mansion.

After tying his horse to a hitching post, he went quickly up the front steps and knocked on the towering front door. So like Richard to have a door this size. Loom over you and intimidate you even before you'd gotten inside.

"Yes, sir. Good evening, sir." This was white-jacketed Carlos. The butler. The man seemed to work twenty-four hours a day.

"I need to see Neville."

"Very good, sir. Wait here and I'll announce you." All with a Mex accent, of course.

But there would be none of that royal bullshit this time. Duncan pushed past Carlos and rushed down the parquet hall leading to the home office Neville preferred to work out of. The place still stank from all the funeral flowers that had been in the front room where the wake — complete with body — had been held.

He didn't knock. He burst in.

Neville, behind his desk, looked up. He was startled for perhaps two seconds. Then he was enraged.

"What the hell do you think you're doing, Duncan?"

"Shut the hell up," Duncan said.

He slammed the door hard enough to make a few of the paintings on the walls dance a little. Then he took the telegram from inside his suit jacket and pitched it onto Neville's desk.

"I asked you what the hell you thought you were doing?" Neville said, not even looking at the telegram.

"And I told you to shut up. And I'm still telling you to shut up. And read that telegram."

Neville had to say something before he read the telegram, of course. His kind always have the last word.

"You're going to regret coming in this way, unannounced. You seem to think you've got some sort of upper hand now, but you don't. And I don't give a damn what that telegram says."

Duncan slid his Peacemaker out from inside his coat.

"Read it, Richard. Now."

"That's just one more thing you're going to regret, Duncan. Pulling a gun on me. You must be losing your mind."

"Read it. Now."

Neville finally picked up the telegram. Unfolded it angrily. Laid it flat upon his desk and scanned it.

Wasn't a long telegram. Didn't take much reading, much time.

"Sonofabitch," Neville said when he finished reading it.

"Those lawyers of yours better know how to save our lives, Richard, or I'm going to cooperate with the law."

Neville, curiously, spoke softly now, almost gently. "We've had our differences, Aaron. But I've always liked you."

"Sure, Richard. You don't like anybody but yourself."

"Will you listen to me? You can't stand there with that ridiculous gun of yours — I'm sorry, Aaron, you just don't look that threatening with a gun in your hand — and tell me that we didn't have some good times when we started hanging around together a couple of years ago. That trip to New Orleans? That trip to St. Louis? Those mulatto girls we found in Cheyenne that time?"

But Duncan wasn't caught up in Neville's attempt at nostalgia.

"We didn't kill people then. The men who died in those fires we had set —"

"It was an accident, Aaron. An accident. It's almost as if you *want* to feel guilty about those men."

Duncan held up his free hand.

"All that matters now is that we figure out how to deal with the insurance company and Prine, Richard. You're supposed to be the smart one here. What the hell are we going to do?"

"I'll tell you one thing we're not going to do," Neville said. "We're not going to start running around in circles and looking like we've got something to hide. You understand that, Aaron?"

Duncan's resolve had been waning. Going up against Neville was just too difficult. He wasn't afraid of the telegram, he wasn't afraid of Duncan's gun. He was a man naturally given to controlling all situations. And this situation was no different.

"Now, will you put that stupid damned gun down here on the desk, Aaron?"

"You really have an idea?" Duncan knew how desperate, childlike, he sounded.

"I really have an idea, but I'm not saying anything else until that Peacemaker of yours is right here on my desk."

Duncan looked and felt defeated. All his life he'd been a secondary figure. Even at the mattress plant. The foreman ran the place day to day. What the hell did Duncan know about mattresses? And the accountant ran everything else. What the hell did Duncan know about running books?

"You're never going to amount to anything," Duncan's father had managed to say virtually every day of Duncan's boyhood. Not good at sports, not good at carpentry or riding horses or baseball — the things his father and his older brothers were all good at. And then to feel so damned sorry for himself. A dozen times a day, Duncan took stock of himself and felt this burden of self-disgust. Men — and women — were right to find him repellent, laughable, weak. He was all those things.

Now he was about to turn over his weapon. He'd come out here in such a fine rage. He was going to take control. He was going to figure out how to deal with the telegram. He was going to show Neville that Aaron Duncan was every bit his equal.

His jaw muscles bunched and unbunched. They were like a tumor just beneath his skin. He leaned forward, set the weapon down on the clean desktop, and pushed it over to Neville.

Where Duncan was indecisive, fearful, confused by it all, Richard Neville was purposeful, unafraid, and single-minded. He knew exactly what he needed and wanted to do, and he did it.

He picked up the Peacemaker and shot Aaron Duncan twice in the chest.

CHAPTER TWENTY-FIVE

"You realize I've just destroyed my husband," Ellie Duncan said as she walked him back to his horse. She'd sobered up some. Probably too much, given everything she'd told Prine over the past half hour. She'd probably need to start drinking again when she realized all the implications of her confession.

"I'm sorry, Ellie."

"I'm scared for him. I don't love him anymore. But I'm scared for him. All the things you hear about prison life —"

She began to cry. "I don't know what I'll tell our children. If they ever find out that I betrayed their father . . ."

He took her gently to him, brushing her hair with his big hand, letting her dampen his shirt with her warm tears.

He headed back to town, riding fast.

I didn't cause her death. Neville did. He paid Tolan and Rooney to kill her. They would've killed her even if I hadn't tried to take advantage of the situation. But, shit, it's

*never going to be the same for me. I saw that
I'm no more honest than half the people I arrest.
Maybe a lot of people would've tried the same
thing I did. Maybe most of us are a lot closer
to being dishonest than we know. I sure as hell
am. And that's going to stay with me the rest
of my life.*

When Carlos came in and saw Duncan's
body on the floor, Richard Neville stopped
what he was doing at his wall safe and said,
"You opened the front door for him, didn't
you?"

"Yessir."

"You saw how angry he was, didn't
you?"

"Yessir."

"I didn't have any choice. He had a
gun."

Carlos seemed confused, obviously realizing that the Peacemaker on the desk did
not belong to his employer.

"That was the gun you used?"

"Yes."

"But it's —"

"It's his gun. And this is where you have
to listen very carefully, Carlos. Do you
understand?"

"Yessir."

"I grabbed his gun from him and started

walking back to my desk. Do you understand so far, Carlos?"

"Yessir."

"But just as I turned my back, he reached inside his coat. I only caught a glimpse of that — but then I heard you shout, 'He's got a gun!'"

"I see, sir. A lie."

"Dammit, it's not a lie. It's exactly what happened."

"Yessir."

"But I'm going to need a little corroboration."

"Corroboration, sir?"

"Yes, Carlos. Corroboration. It means somebody swearing that that's what happened. Somebody vouching for me. You understand?"

"Now I do. Yessir."

"You'd heard us arguing — Duncan and I — and you rushed in to see if everything was all right. You saw me wrestle the gun from him. And when I got it and started back to my desk, you saw him — from the back — reach into his jacket and start to pull something out. That's when you shouted that he had a gun. Now, can you remember all that?"

"Yessir."

Carlos raised his gaze to the open wall safe.

"I'm going on an overnight trip. Some extremely important business. You ride into town and tell Sheriff Daly what happened out here. And tell him I'll be back sometime tomorrow."

"But shouldn't you be here, Mr. Neville? A dead man — it will not look so good if you're not here."

Neville could feel himself swell with rage. He was not used to his servants arguing with him. But anger would only irritate Carlos more.

Neville said, "Carlos, I'm asking you to help me. I have a very important meeting I need to attend. A great deal depends on this meeting. Your job included. Do you understand?"

"Yessir."

"So I need you to do exactly as I say. All right?"

Carlos, too, had apparently decided that challenging his boss was not the best way to proceed.

"Yessir."

"I need the three suits I had made in Chicago packed right away. With all the appropriate shirts and cravats and so on. Just as if you were packing for me on an extended trip. All right?"

"Yessir."

"And I need you to do it now. Right now."

"Yessir."

Carlos wasted no time. He gave a half-bow and removed himself from the office.

The gringos have their laws. Very complicated laws. Neville, he killed Mr. Duncan. He is guilty of murder. By gringo law, I will be guilty of helping him if I lie for him. Gringo law makes provision for that. They have a word for that. Accessory. I could go to prison. Neville, he would not give a damn. Not about me or about my Maria or my three children. When he fires people on a whim, he does not care that they may not find work again for a very long time. Look at Juan. Seven months, and still no job. And when I asked Neville about hiring him back — Juan did nothing; Neville just had one of his stupid hangovers and was in a mood to bully someone — he said that if I ever brought up the subject again, he would fire me on the spot. But he will also fire me if I don't pack his clothes. And lie for him when I bring back Daly and Prine. Blessed Mother, help me to know the right thing to do. The rich gringos, they do not care for us. You and Jesus are our only friends in this terrible world of rich gringos. Our only friends.

★ ★ ★

By the time Prine reached the sheriff's office, Bob Carlyle was gone for the day and Sheriff Daly was waiting for Harry Ryan to relieve him for the night. Deep shadow and a dusk sky streaked the colors of rose and sunflowers lent elegance to the hurry-home, scurry-home rush of downtown workers. It was just chill enough that even the office coffee smelled good.

Daly was working on paperwork. He looked up and said, "Was wonderin' where you'd got to."

"We need to get out to Neville's place."

Daly put his pen down. "Any special reason?"

"Neville hired Tolan and Rooney to kill Cassie. He's lost a lot of money on bad investments. He needed her half of the fortune."

Daly whistled. "You sure about all this? Because if you aren't, Neville's gonna run out straight up the map into Canada. That is, if he don't decide to shoot us first."

"I just spent forty-five minutes talking to Ellie Duncan. Aaron and Neville burned those three businesses down. Neville was the silent partner I was trying to find."

"Maybe Neville killed Al Woodward, too."

"That's a possibility. For sure."

Daly levered himself up from the desk chair.

"Old man Neville's turning over in his grave. You hear him?"

Prine smiled. "Yeah, I hear him."

"Probably should take my shotgun, huh?"

"Probably wouldn't be a bad idea."

Richard Neville never knew exactly how much cash he had on hand. There was less than he'd hoped in the wall safe. It didn't even bulk out of the sides of the Gladstone bag he put it in. By his count, he had eight thousand dollars in there. No pittance, to be sure. But not enough for him to retire, either.

He walked to the door of the den and shouted up the stairs.

"As soon as you're done, Carlos, bring that suitcase down here."

"Yessir."

Yessir. Sometimes Neville wondered if that was the only English word Carlos knew. Mexes in general and Carlos in particular profoundly irritated Neville. He figured they saw themselves — unlike Indians or colored people — as pretty close to white. Which meant they made the best

servants but that they were the most difficult to deal with because they thought they
were just as good as the whites.

Another irritant was the way Aaron
Duncan's corpse had begun to smell. My
God, what a coarse, filthy stench. One
more reason he'd be glad to get out of
here.

Carlos said, "It is ready."

A large leather box was what the suitcase
looked like. This was the one Neville took
for all his long trips. And this was certainly
going to be a long one. Forever.

"Good. Now get the buggy ready and
bring it around front."

"Yessir."

There it was again. Yessir. A parrot was
what he was. Smart enough to pick up a
few words. But not smart enough to pick
up anything more.

"And then wait an hour and ride in and
tell Daly what happened."

"Yessir."

"You remember what we agreed on?"

"Yessir."

"And quit saying 'yessir.' "

Carlos seemed confused.

"I am not to call you 'sir' any more?"

"The 'sir' is fine. Just don't put the 'yes'
in front of it."

"In front? I do not understand."

Neville cursed. What a ridiculous conversation. He needed to concentrate on getting out of here. Running the buggy as fast as it would go. Picking up the train in the morning and heading out. No way he could catch the train in Claybank. Too easy for Daly to find him if he did.

"What the hell're you standing there for?" Neville snapped. "Get the buggy ready and bring it around."

Carlos vanished from the doorway.

Chapter Twenty-six

"You wanted to talk to me about something the other day, remember?" Daly said as they rode at a fast and steady pace to Neville's on the dusty stage road that wound around small hills and stands of hardwood. They both wore their sheepskins. When they talked their breath was pure silver against the shadows.

Did Prine remember? The morning he'd wanted to tell Daly all about the role he'd played in Cassie's murder, his stomach had been so twisted up, his bowels so cold and slithery, and his sweat so hot and dirty — well, he sure as hell wasn't going to forget that for a while.

Prine nodded. "Yeah, I remember. But everything worked out all right."

Even in the moonlight, a tatter of gray cloud obscuring some of the light, Prine could feel Daly's eyes on him.

Daly was a smart old bastard. He might not have known what kind of crisis Prine had been living through. But he'd known it was a crisis and not just some piddling little trivial matter.

"You learn anything from it?"

"Pardon?"

"You learn anything from it? That's the only way you get any better at things. To learn from your mistakes or your problems. Take Hettie over to the saloon."

"What about her?"

Hettie was a vivacious forty-year-old who was woman enough to attract men and rough enough to keep unruly gamblers in their place.

"Couple years ago, she asked me if I wanted to come up to her apartment one rainy night. I think you can pretty much tell what she had in mind."

"Did you go?"

"Damned right I went."

"Your wife ever find out?"

"Yeah."

"Somebody told her, huh?"

"Yeah, me."

"You? Why'd you tell her?"

"Because I owed her the truth, Prine. I went up there, all right. But as soon as we started drinking, Hettie crowded up next to me on the couch. And I crowded her right back. But just as I started to kiss her, I stopped. I thought of how this one night was going to change my whole life. The wife and I have always been honest with each other. But I couldn't be honest about this. Not ever. There'd always be this one lie, this one secret between us. And I couldn't do it. I learned right then that my wife was the most important person in my life and that I'd be a damned fool to step out on her this way. I went home and told her, and we had a couple of drinks and a good long laugh about it and then we picked up just where Hettie and I'd left off."

"That sounds like a Bible lesson."

Daly laughed. "Yeah, but I doubt a preacher man'd ever let you know that he was up in Hettie's apartment."

Carlos was just hefting the suitcase into the shallow bed of the buggy when he heard riders approaching.

He ran to the edge of the grass for a better look. Two riders limned by moonlight, dust the color of fading ghosts as they turned in toward the estate.

One of the men jerked his carbine from his saddle scabbard, the barrel gleaming in the moonsilver.

He turned away and ran back into the house.

Prine, carbine ready, said, "I'm going in the house."

"You in charge now, are you?" Daly said. He sounded amused.

"I can move faster."

"That you can," Daly said as they reined up. "I'll work my way around back. In case he tries to get out that way."

Prine dropped from his horse, leaving him ground-tied.

He moved fast, crouched down.

Something white moved on the shadows of the front porch.

"Come out of there," Prine snapped.

"He killed a man in there, Deputy. I am afraid to go back in."

"Carlos? Come out here where I can see you."

Carlos came up, his arms stuck straight up above his head. His white serving jacket rode up to his ribs.

"Where is he?" Prine said.

"Getting ready to leave. The den, I think."

"Now tell me about what happened in there. Who'd he kill?"

Sheriff Daly made his way around to the back of the house. It was like walking around a stadium in a big city. A man could lose some weight just making the trek.

Weight wasn't his only problem, Daly thought. He had arthritis, bursitis, and neuritis. He probably had all the other itises, too, if he ever bothered to go back to the doc. He'd busted his knee once, so he hobbled a bit; and he needed new eyeglasses, so he squinted a bit; and he was fighting a mild case of shingles, which kept him in minor but constant pain. He was one hell of a specimen, he was, and he was damned glad that Prine had suggested going in first.

Daly took up his position at the back door, next to the screened-in porch. Either way, Neville wasn't going to escape. He'd protected the Nevilles for twenty years. But no longer. He was now — at last — an emancipated white man.

Prine moved carefully through the house. He remembered from his single visit here where the den was.

He stood to the side of the door and said, "Neville, this is Prine. I need you to come out with your hands up."

For a time, the only sound was the tocking of a grandfather clock and the relentless pounding of his own heart. He was oily with sweat. He was trembling.

"Neville. Make this easy for both of us."

"How's it feel, Prine? You get to come into the mansion and arrest the richest man in the valley."

"If you're so rich, why did you have to burn down those three buildings and then have your sister murdered by Tolan and Rooney?"

The silence again.

"If you were sensible, we could talk about this."

"I'm not sensible, Neville. So don't even bother to try and pay me off."

The shotgun blast packed the air with buckshot and a roaring echo. A large chunk of the solid oak den door was torn out.

"You try to get in here, Prine, you know what you'll be facing. I keep a lot of ammunition in here."

Prine was worrying a plan. If he could quickly try and kick the door open, kick it back on its hinges so he'd have a clear shot, and then fall to the floor where Neville would have a difficult time seeing him for a moment or two — maybe he could get a shot off that way. He wanted to take Neville alive. He wanted to attend the hanging.

He needed to make Neville nervous. Silence was his ally. He began to make his move, walking on tiptoe, moving himself in position to try and kick in the door and then dive for the floor in case Neville was standing on the other side with his shotgun ready.

Apparently, Neville was practicing silence too. Trying to unnerve Prine. Not a sound in the den.

Prine took a couple of deep breaths. Everything depended on timing. If he was caught in the center of the door on this side, Neville would have no trouble killing him.

He moved. There was no thought process now. No time for it. He acted strictly on instinct and a terrified need to survive.

He brought his boot up and kicked at a place just above the doorknob. The door swung backward with such force that it sounded as if an explosion had just taken place.

This was where Prine expected the shotgun to erupt. He didn't doubt Neville's word that he had a lot of ammunition.

He dropped to the floor, his Winchester ready to fire.

A sound. But not of a shotgun. A faint squeaking noise — something being opened.

As he lay there on the floor, ready to

belly-crawl inside, he pictured the den. The large desk, globe, the immensity of built-in bookcases — the mullioned windows.

That was the sound he'd just heard.

The huge, mullioned, palace-like mullioned windows being opened.

An easy way for Neville to escape.

No wonder there hadn't been the sound of a shotgun. Or Neville shouting at him.

Neville was no longer in the den.

He was just jumping to his feet when the brutal charge of the shotgun troubled the autumn night. Then — a cry. Somebody shot. Somebody down.

Prine ran to the back of the house, not knowing exactly how to find the back door. A couple of false turns before he found the steps next to the pantry leading down to the landing and the back door.

He took the steps quickly. He'd already formed a picture of what he was going to see. And that was what he did indeed see when he reached the enormous backyard.

Sheriff Daly was on the grass, on his back, blood soaking the front of his shirt. He'd opened his sheepskin, apparently to get some air. People did off things when they'd been wounded mortally.

Two shots from the garage where the

buggies were kept. The horses were in the adjacent barn.

Prine dove to the ground and rolled to the right, over to Daly. Two more shots, both nearly hitting him. The frost soaked his Levi's. He ended up with his jaw resting on a dog turd.

Prine put four shots into the dark garage. He knew he'd come close by the way Neville cursed him. Neville obviously needed to get into the barn. Get a horse. Get out of here. He'd likely brought a lot more ammunition than Prine did. Eventually, this would make Neville invincible unless Prine got lucky and shot him. He had no more thought — not after seeing poor Daly dead or dying — of taking Neville in. He wanted him to die. And he wanted to be the man who killed him.

Prine, almost without realizing it, started rolling again. He wished he'd gotten rid of his sheepskin. It was pretty damned bulky.

Several more shots from Neville. Each one progressively closer. The family dog, wherever it was, was now barking along with the shots. Apparently, it felt that they were holding another recital here and it, naturally enough, wanted to join in.

Prine got where he'd wanted to go. Out of Neville's range. He got to his feet and raced around the far side of the barn. The stark smell of horseshit; the slippery feel of hay on the floor. Four horses in stalls, each awake now and casting sidelong glances at the strange human running past them with a Winchester in his hand.

He hurried through the barn to the doors. It was his intention to ease himself out and then sneak across to the garage. He would surprise Neville and this would at last be done.

He began his quiet move from barn to garage. The horses had settled down some. He could hear the night again.

He pressed himself flat against the front side of the garage. He began moving inch by inch. When he reached the open door, he would duck down and pick off Neville in the darkness.

He was halfway to the open door when he heard somebody say, "Your turn to come out with your hands up, asshole."

Easy enough to see what had happened, Prine thought. Easy enough to see that I didn't think he'd do the same thing I did. Easy enough to see he's going to kill me.

Neville held the shotgun level with Prine's chest and then moved slowly around so that his back was to the house.

"I almost thought we were going to be

friends someday," Neville said.

"Yeah. I like being friends with men who get their sisters murdered."

"There wasn't any pleasure in it for me, Prine. I did it because I had to. I wasn't particularly fond of her, but I didn't especially want to see her get killed." He shook his head. "Now, you're another matter. First thing you did when we got back to town was start to build a case against me. First damned thing. And I have to say that really pissed me off, Prine. It really did. So shooting you isn't going to be tough at all. Not at all."

He'd been so caught up in his own words, Neville, that he didn't see what was going on behind him.

Sheriff Daly rising from the dead, or something very much like it, and picking up his fallen Winchester and taking several tortured, half-stumbled steps so he'd be sure to be in range —

And then just blasting the shit out of Neville. Just blasting the shit right out of him.

Chapter Twenty-seven

You could barely get into Daly's tiny hospital room for all the good stuff people had brought him. You had flowers, you had several boxes of candy, you had enough magazines to give you cataracts, you had new shirts, new jeans, new boots, a new hairbrush, and on and on.

And you had Lucy.

She was in his room every chance she got. They had this odd sort of crush on each other, and Prine didn't care at all.

He'd sit there and watch Daly flirt with her and then watch her flirt right back. And all he'd do was smile.

All this passed, of course, in time.

Daly left the hospital — he still had bursitis and all the other itises, but his shooting arm was all right again, anyway — and Lucy and Prine got married, and Lucy in the middle of the night woke up one time and knew that she was with child. And Bob Carlyle retired from being deputy. And Daly decided it was time for him to retire, too, so Prine was made sheriff.

He needed the raise in pay. That October, Lucy got pregnant again.

About the Author

Ed Gorman has been called "one of suspense fiction's best storytellers" by *Ellery Queen*, and "one of the most original voices in today's crime fiction" by the *San Diego Union*.

Gorman's work has appeared in magazines as various as *Redbook*, *Ellery Queen*, *The Magazine of Fantasy and Science Fiction*, and *Poetry Today*.

His work has won numerous prizes, including the Shamus, the Spur, and the International Fiction Writer's awards. He's been nominated for the Edgar, the Anthony, the Golden Dagger, and the Bram Stoker awards.

Former *Los Angeles Times* critic Charles Champlin noted that "Ed Gorman is a powerful storyteller."

Gorman's work has been taken by the Literary Guild, The Mystery Guild, Doubleday Book Club, and the Science Fiction Book Club.